The Christmas Guest

Daisy Bell lives in south London. She loves baking gingerbread and decorating the Christmas tree, but always leaves the gift-wrapping until the last possible moment!

The Christmas Guest

DAISY BELL

Quercus

First published in Great Britain in 2016 by

Quercus Publishing Ltd
Carmelite House
50 Victoria Embankment
London EC4Y 0DZ

An Hachette UK company

A CIP catalogue record for this book is available
from the British Library.

HB ISBN 978 1 78648 171 9
EBOOK ISBN 978 1 78648 173 3

10 9 8 7 6 5 4 3 2 1

Typeset by CC Book Production
Printed and bound in Great Britain by Clays Ltd, St Ives plc.

*For my daughter,
and to Max, Lara and all the puppies
we had over the years*

✳ *Prologue* ✳

'I want to go home.'

There, I've said it. Not that there's anybody around to hear me; I haven't seen a human for ages now, let alone a fellow dog. I've been trying to put on a brave face for the past few hours, but I'm beginning to think that my brilliant plan may not have been quite so brilliant after all. In fact, it could well be the silliest thing I've ever done – and I've already made quite a few mistakes during my two short months on this earth.

This morning when I made my great escape, I thought that running off to explore the world would be a fantastic adventure, and to start with I guess it *was* fun. OK, there were a few hairy moments – like wandering a little too close to that huge road with its terrifying roar of traffic and trying to befriend those gigantic animals with the scary-looking horns that nearly trampled me when I wriggled under their fence to say hello – but to be free to run and romp and scamper after being shut inside for nearly all my young life made me literally giddy with joy. And, oh my goodness, the *smells*! No sooner had I caught one delicious scent, my nose was leading me off on some other tantalising trail, sending me zigzagging all over the place, my tail wagging so hard it almost knocked me jaws over paws. Yes, in those first few heady moments, my heart beating wildly with the boundless potential of my new-found freedom, I felt happier and more alive than ever before.

But now my legs are wobbly with exhaustion, I'm cold, there's an ache of emptiness in my tummy – and, worse, in my heart. The world is turning out to be a far bigger and scarier place than I could ever have imagined, and I'm realising just how little I know about how it all works. How do I find food if it's not presented to me in a bowl? Where can I sleep tonight? And how do you even *start* to look for a new family to love? Yes, I'm afraid this is turning out to be a very big mistake indeed, but then Mum always did say that my nose for adventure would lead me into trouble.

I've been wandering along this narrow, twisty lane, bordered by high hedgerows, for some time now, hoping it will lead me somewhere where there are friendly humans, but it's beginning to get dark and I need to find shelter for the night. It's very cold and the thought of sleeping out in the open, all alone, is terrifying. This place – wherever I am – with its trees and grass and endless space and silence is so different to the city where I lived before. There it was never quiet, not even in the very dead of night when most humans are asleep. I think this place must be the countryside; at least, that's what Veronica called it as she bundled me into the car this morning.

'We're going to stay with my parents in the country-side for Christmas,' she had said, shoving me into the tiny gap between all the suitcases. 'So you better be on your best behaviour, Mr Snuffles.'

Ah yes, I'm afraid that's the name she gave me: Mr Snuffles. I *know*. Even her husband, Richard, didn't think it was a good idea.

'He's a white golden retriever, Veronica; he's going to

grow up to be a big dog. You can't call him Mr Snuffles, it's not fair.' But Veronica wanted the name – and, as I quickly learned, whatever Veronica wanted, she got.

In the distance I hear the ominous rushing noise that signals a car is approaching. I now know to jump out of the way, after an earlier near-miss that left me shaking and soaked in muddy water and turned my bright white coat a far less impressive shade of dirty brown. I cower in the hedgerow as the car flashes past, its lights briefly dazzling me. Even after the danger has passed I'm still trembling, so I stay where I am for a moment to calm myself before venturing out to face the world again. *Come on, Puppy, be brave* . . .

Then, suddenly, I hear a sound in the undergrowth nearby and catch the scent of something irresistible. Despite my exhaustion, I wriggle under the hedgerow following my twitching nose and find myself at the edge of another expanse of grass, although this time, to my delight, there are signs of human life: paths, flower beds, a playground and, in the distance, a scattering of buildings. It's nowhere near as built-up as the city I came from, but where there are humans there is food, and maybe shelter too. And then – oh joy! – in the rapidly falling darkness I spot another dog accompanied by its owner and they're heading in my direction. I give a few excited barks in greeting and a few moments later the dog has come bounding up to me, ball in jaws.

He's a black and tan terrier about my size, even though he's fully grown. He drops the ball in front of him.

'Hey kid, are you lost?'

I'm not sure how to answer. 'I'm on an adventure,' I eventually reply with as much swagger as I can muster. 'I'm exploring the world.'

'But where are your humans?'

'I . . . I ran away from them.' Just saying the words makes me feel like whimpering at my foolishness. I sit down, trying to be strong, trying to keep myself together. 'We were in the car travelling to the country-side, you see, and then my humans stopped to let me out for a quick break and I just . . . kept running.'

The terrier cocks his head to one side questioningly. 'But why? Did they mistreat you?'

'No, but . . .' I think back to the weeks I spent with Veronica and Richard: the plush-cushioned bed they gave me to sleep in, the plentiful bowls of puppy food, the clothes Veronica tried (and failed) to dress me in, including a bright pink jacket which was far too tight around my tummy and itched horribly, although at least its little gold buttons were fun to chew off. At first there were cuddles too: she wouldn't stop stroking and kissing me when I arrived, and while I still desperately missed my mother and the rest of my litter I began to feel loved and safe again. But then, somehow, everything went disastrously wrong.

The terrier's human is calling him. 'Oops, sorry, got to go,' he says before I can say more. 'Good luck with your adventure, kid. Look after yourself, it's going to be a chilly night.' And with that he picks up the ball and dashes off just as quickly as he appeared.

For a split second I think about chasing after him to ask if I can go home with him or even just play for a while, but he's already quite a long way away and I'm too tired to catch up with him. I sink to the ground and put my head on my paws, trying not to cry. I just want to go home! But where *is* my home? I don't suppose I have one any more. And with that realisation, my heart lurches horribly.

There's a bitterly chill wind and my fur is still damp from its earlier drenching by the car. If I've got to spend the night outside, I really should find somewhere to shelter or else I'll freeze. Picking myself up and giving myself a shake, I wander down the path in the direction of the distant buildings. I don't think they're human houses – they're too small and they don't have any lights on – but whatever they are, hopefully I can find a way to crawl inside to warm up. There's nobody else around now, but I hear occasional scrabbling sounds in the bushes and catch glimpses of movement beneath the trees. I'd usually be keen to investigate further, but being alone in the dark suddenly feels rather menacing, so I stick to the path and pick up my pace. Although it's now completely dark, I notice that my shadow is still trotting along next to me and I look up to find a dazzling full moon. I stop and stare up at its familiar silvery face, which I'd often admired through the windows of Veronica's house, and, with a surge of courage, I realise that I don't feel quite so alone any more.

Then, as I watch, something white and sparkling begins to drift from the sky, as if fragments of the moon are falling to earth. At first just a few float down, but then more and more appear, filling the air like the white feathers that once stuffed the plump cushions of my bed – and even the memory of Veronica's furious scolding at *that* particular incident can't spoil the magic of this moment. Spellbound, I watch as one of the moonflakes drifts lazily towards my nose . . . Oof, that tickles! I shake my head, then sneeze so hard I tumble over. Yikes, this stuff is cold! I really *do* need to find some shelter . . .

Nearby, I spot a bench in front of a hedge. Abandoning the idea of reaching the distant buildings, I decide the darkness underneath looks like a cosy enough space for a small puppy, so I crawl in and am overjoyed to be rewarded with the half-eaten remains of a ham sandwich. It's a bit muddy and only a mouthful, but right now it tastes amazing.

Curling up beneath the bench, I stare out and watch the magical white stuff swirl and tumble through the air and, as I tuck my paws into my tummy trying to get warm, I'm suddenly hit by an overwhelming memory of being snuggled up with my mother. Just the thought of her brings with it a powerful sensation of warmth and happiness and safety, a feeling of being home, of being truly loved. I wonder if I'll ever feel like that again?

I've been trying so hard to be brave, but now, curled up under that bench, lost and alone, I finally allow myself to despair. I'm just so tired . . . My eyelids are growing heavier now and as they shut the last thing I see is the moon dust beginning to settle on the grass, turning it silvery-white, transforming the world into an even stranger and more mysterious place.

❄ *Eight Days Until Christmas* ❄

I wake with a start. For a second I'm confused: where am I? Why aren't I in bed in Veronica and Richard's kitchen? But then an avalanche of uncomfortable sensations – cold, hunger, fear – reminds me exactly where I am, and I remember the not-so-brilliant plan that landed me here.

Lifting my head, I warily peer out from under the bench. It's very dark now, the moon must be hidden behind the clouds. The white stuff has stopped falling from the sky, but there's now a thick layer of it covering the ground, plumped up like the duvet on Richard and Veronica's bed, smothering all the world's smells and sounds. It's so beautiful that for a moment I forget my troubles and simply gaze at the magical landscape, before a horrible, screeching yowl shatters the stillness, sending terror shooting through me. My ears prick up: what in dog's name was that? It sounds like something big, wild – and hungry. As I wriggle further under the bench there's an answering cry, only this time it comes from closer by. I wait, frozen in panic, my eyes scanning the dark for signs of movement and my nose twitching at the faint but unmistakable scent of danger, but the world has grown silent again, save for the rapid panting of my breath. I'm shivering uncontrollably – is it from the cold or from fear? I might be hidden from view here, but I feel as exposed as if I were out in the open. The darkness and that terrible howling has made me more conscious than ever that I'm still just a little puppy and out here on my own. Surely I can find a safer place than this to spend the rest of the night?

I struggle upright, but tumble jaws over paws again; the cold has made me stiff and besides I still haven't quite mastered my legs. I think I've got the hang of them, but then I grow a bit bigger and suddenly they don't work like I want them to. Mum always used to tell me to take things slowly, to be patient, that I'll grow into myself in time ... The thought of her starts me crying again. *If Mum was here, she'd know what to do. No, you mustn't think like that. You got yourself into this; you need to find a way out of it.*

My tummy growls, reminding me that my last proper meal was breakfast – that morsel of sandwich barely made a dent in my hunger. Cautiously, I creep out from under the bench, hoping that whatever was making that noise has by now moved on. I can't smell it any more either, so I assume that I'm safe – for now, anyway. It's too dark to see anything clearly, so I stick my nose up in the air, hoping that it will guide me in the right direction. As I sniff the chill air I catch wind of a scent that makes my tail quiver and my tummy turn somersaults of anticipation. I know that smell! I remember it from Richard and Veronica's house. *That* is the smell of roast chicken. I remember the taste too. Veronica had fed bits to me under the table, and it was the most heavenly thing I had ever tasted. My jaws begin to water at the memory: crispy skin, soft, buttery meat ... Suddenly I no longer care about the cold or dark, or strange, screeching animals. Wherever that roast chicken is, that's where I want to be!

With a rush of energy I bound forward – and promptly plunge up to my whiskers in a huge pile of the white stuff. Whoops . . . Struggling back to my paws, covered in it from nose to tail, I give myself a shake to get the worst off. Some of it has even got on my tongue, and while I'm trying to spit it out I'm amazed to discover that it has turned into fresh water in my mouth. I haven't had a drink in ages, so I lick up some more. Brrrr, this moon dust is freezing! There's such a thick layer of it that it almost reaches up to my tummy when I'm standing. I lift a paw experimentally and gently put it down again, watching with interest as it disappears into the white blanket. Now I try taking a few steps, but immediately stumble. Hmmm, this is not going to make progress very easy . . . Perhaps if I crouch down to give me an extra boost, I can spring forward with both paws and then . . . *Yes!* This time I manage to stay upright. Success!

So I set off on the trail of the scent, adopting a bouncing sort of bunny hop instead of my usual trot. All the crouching and springing is very tiring and I'm dizzy with hunger, but the chicken smell works like magic, distracting me from my frozen paws and empty tummy and urging me on, until far off in the distance I spot a speck of light. Could it be . . .? Yes, it appears to be coming from a house! It's still a long way off, but I'm pretty sure if I can get there, that's where I'll find the roast chicken.

I try to pick up the pace, my breath turning to fog in the crisp air as I huff and puff through the snow. Although I have to stop now and then to sneeze my whiskers clean and shake the snow from my eyelashes. I'm flagging, stumbling more often now, but I'm heartened by the fact that the smell is growing stronger. The scent brings with it the promise not only of food, but of a warm kitchen and (*is it too much to hope for?*) a loving family with room in their home and their hearts for a small-ish, obedient-ish puppy. Because surely nothing bad could happen in a place that smells this good? Perhaps the family might even have some children of their own for me to play with . . . The possibility of new pals to tumble around with is almost as exciting as the prospect of food, and drives me forward. I haven't really had anyone to play with since leaving my brothers and sisters – and how long ago was that now? I find it very tricky to keep track of time, but I do know how old I am because I heard Veronica telling one of her friends the other day. 'He's two months old and into *everything*,' she had said with a roll of her eyes. (I'm not sure what she meant, but I got the impression that it wasn't something she was particularly happy about.) Two months isn't a very long time, I know, but so much has happened since then that I feel like I've already lived a lifetime.

My earliest memory is of cuddling up with my litter-mates, jostling to be the closest to our mum. To begin with, this was all I knew – warmth, milk, a comforting lick from Mum, the odd nip from one of my siblings – but as the world came into focus I discovered an urge to explore, to investigate what lay beyond our cosy nest. My curiosity was further sparked by a succession of interesting-smelling human visitors, and I would make sure I was always the first to greet them with a friendly lick and wagging tail. I was perfectly content with my place in our little pack and had no reason to think that life would ever be any different.

The day when everything changed began with a visit

from a man we hadn't met before. He was very tall, with a calm sort of manner (humans tended to be quite excitable when they met us for the first time), and was far better groomed than other humans we'd seen, in a blue jacket and matching trousers with a strange red thing tied around his neck – a sort of lead, perhaps? The man's fur was dark brown, brushed to a shine, his skin was a lovely golden colour and his eyes sparkled. I overheard him tell our human, a nice lady called Jean, that he had 'just come back from the Maldives'. I got the impression this had something to do with the colour of his skin. (As I've mentioned before, I have always been quite a nosy puppy.) Anyway, when Jean brought him over to meet us I boldly wriggled my way to the front of the box to say hello. Perhaps I should have kept myself hidden away with Mum like my littlest sister always did, then I wouldn't be in this mess now, but at the time I was just proud that I was the first to be picked up and fussed over by this smart-looking man. Of course, I was well used to being handled by humans by this time, but on this particular occasion the man didn't return me to Mum. Instead, Jean dropped me into a strange basket and the door was fastened shut.

At first I was curious, exploring my new surroundings, having an experimental nibble of the bars, but after a while I began to get a little panicky. The basket smelled strange and I couldn't find a way to get out. Although I could still smell Mum, I could no longer see where she was. I began to whimper, sure that she would come and rescue me, but then I felt the basket move, and the scent of Mum gradually grew weaker until there was the sound of a door shutting and I had no sense of her at all.

By now I was terrified. *What was happening? Where was I going?* I was trapped in the basket, shaking with fear. I couldn't see much through the bars, but after a few moments I felt the basket being set down, another door slammed, and then a strange rumbling began that made my tummy go giddy. I didn't know it at the time, but I was on my first car journey.

At first, the man – it was Richard, I know now – tried to comfort me as we drove.

'Shhh. It's OK, Puppy, no need to cry. We're going to your new home.'

But although I tried to be brave, I was still very young and thought that if I shouted loud enough Mum would be able to find me. Eventually Richard gave up trying to calm me and instead turned on the radio, drowning out the sound of my cries.

I'm not sure how long we were in the car, but I must have fallen asleep because the next thing I knew Richard's hand was reaching inside the basket to pull me out.

'Well, what a big fuss for a little chap!' he told me, ruffling my fur. 'That wasn't so bad, was it?'

I was in a house, but this place was nothing like Jean's cosily cluttered home. It had a cold, hard floor and high ceilings, and nearly everything I could see – the walls, floors, furniture – was as pure white as my fur. Richard gave me some food, which made me feel a bit happier, and then tied a pale blue ribbon around my neck, which most definitely did *not*. I tried to reach round and tug it off, but the floor was so slippery that I kept skidding and tumbling over. Richard watched me, chuckling to himself.

'Oh, Veronica is going to love you,' he said softly.

Then from somewhere in the house I heard a door slam and a woman's voice.

'Darling, I'm home! Rich? Are you here?'

19

He scooped me up and held me in front of him, looking into my eyes.

'Right then, Puppy, are you ready to meet your new mummy?'

Tucking me under his arm he carried me along a corridor and into another huge room – again all white – where a young woman was standing looking at what I now know is called a mobile phone. I stopped wriggling for a moment and stared at her. She was just so . . . *shiny.* Her fur was a shimmering gold colour, her face all glowy as if she were made of sunshine, and she had sparkly things hanging from her ears and more decorating her fingers. Whereas Jean was shaped like a ball, this lady was all stretched out – her legs seemed to go on for ever – and for one astonishing moment I thought that she was covered with white fur just like me, but then I realised she was wearing a coat. (As I've said, I was still very young at this point, and thought humans had fur coats too!)

The woman glanced up, and when she saw me in Richard's arms her eyes grew wide, she squealed with delight and she broke into the most beautiful smile, which made my heart leap with hope and soothed my desperate longing for home. I started to fidget in Richard's arms, frantically trying to get to this gorgeous human.

'Happy birthday, sweetheart,' said Richard, passing me into her eagerly outstretched arms.

I covered her face with excited licks, feeling increasingly sure that this woman – my 'new mummy' – would love me as much as I knew I could love her. The memory of that morning's ordeal began to fade as she cuddled me, telling me over and over again how handsome I was and how much fun we were going to have together.

'Take a photo, will you, darling – I need one for Instagram,' said Veronica, passing Richard her phone and then holding me up so I was snuggled against her cheek. 'My fur-baby's first Instagram!' she giggled as I nuzzled her face.

The photo-taking took quite a long time; Veronica seemed concerned we should get the perfect shot. As Richard held up the phone at us she posed on the sofa, holding me in the air, then sat on the floor with me on her knees and then stood in front of the window while kissing me. It was all very strange and exciting and I'm afraid to admit, being a very young puppy, I forgot where I was and had a little accident.

'Oh my God!' screeched Veronica, staring in her horror at the damp patch on her top. 'Isn't he house-trained?'

And then she dropped me. I'm sure she didn't mean to, and luckily she was standing on a rug rather than the hard floor so it was a fairly soft landing, and she *did* seem very sorry afterwards, smothering my fur with kisses and telling me that Mummy was very clumsy but she'd never, ever hurt me again . . . but perhaps I should have realised then that this wasn't going to be quite the happy ending I was hoping for.

And so began my new life with Richard and Veronica. At first I had the run of the place, skittering around after Veronica on those slippery floors – marble, I learned it was called – and even being allowed to sleep next to her in bed when Richard was away, which seemed to be quite often. In fact, after that first car journey together I hardly ever saw him. He left the house very early in the morning and came home late at night. 'Daddy has to work very hard at the office to buy nice things for us,' Veronica explained to me.

Veronica went out a lot as well, and to start with she took me with her. I well remember our first outing. It was the day after I went to live with them, and when Veronica told me we were going out to meet her friend for coffee I was so excited I began to bounce around the room in anticipation. Finally, I would get to investigate those intriguing sounds and smells that I'd caught hints of through the windows! But just as we were about to leave the house, instead of letting me walk Veronica scooped me up and put me into her handbag. It was so frustrating! Here I was, venturing outside at long last, but instead of being able to sniff and scamper on the ground I was stuck dangling from Veronica's shoulder. I couldn't see much from inside the bag and there was something knobbly in there with me digging into my tummy, so I tried to shift position and get comfy but Veronica got cross with me for that, so after a while I began chewing the bag's strap out of boredom – but that made her angry too.

Thankfully, when we got to the café Veronica took me out and put me on the ground, but as my lead was looped around the leg of her chair I couldn't go any further than the edge of the table. I wanted nothing more than to be a good puppy and make Veronica proud, but I was bubbling over with energy and desperate to explore, so I began to whine and tug at the lead, which earned me another telling-off.

Then, however, Veronica's friend arrived – and to my delight she had a dog with her too, a small golden poodle, who was also being carried in a handbag.

'Hello.' I smiled, wagging my tail excitedly, desperate to make a friend who might be able to explain how things worked in this confusing human world.

The poodle eyed me suspiciously from inside her bag, which had been placed next to me on the ground. 'Are you new?' she asked.

'Um, I suppose I am, yes.' I gave her bag a friendly sniff. 'Do you like sitting in there?'

'Of course,' said the poodle. 'It's Louis Vuitton.'

'Oh right . . .' I said, trying to look as if I understood what that meant. 'I'd actually quite like to walk rather than being, you know, carried. I haven't been outside much before – well, ever really! There's just so much I want to explore . . .' I realised that I was gabbling so I sat down, trying to be more like my sophisticated new friend. 'Do you live nearby?'

But the poodle ignored my question. 'Your coat looks like it needs a lot of brushing,' she said. 'Which grooming parlour do you frequent?'

I had no idea what she was talking about, so I gave my ear a good scratch while I worked out how to respond, but the poodle shot me a disdainful look and disappeared inside her bag, and I had to occupy myself by chewing my lead until it was time to go home.

After that Veronica took me out with her a few more times and I tried to be on my best behaviour, but in the end she got so grumpy when I wouldn't sit quietly that our outings abruptly stopped. From then on, whenever Veronica went shopping or to meet friends I was left at home with Shirley, an older lady with a cross-looking face who lived in a room at the very top of the house. It took me a while to work out how she fitted into the family, but in time I learned that she was the 'housekeeper'. Her job was to make sure the floors were shiny and the white rooms stayed white – and I'm afraid she didn't like me at all.

'What do they need a bloody dog for?' I heard her

muttering soon after I arrived. 'They're never even at home! And it'll be muggins here who'll end up looking up after it when her ladyship gets bored.'

I stayed out of Shirley's way as much as I could and hoped that in time she would learn to love me.

So the weeks passed and I tried to adapt to my new life in the house, working off my energy by dashing up and down the corridors, but as I got older the urge to go outside grew ever stronger. Although I was let out into the garden a few times a day it was a very small space, with no grass or trees to sniff, so there wasn't much to explore and certainly no room to run. At least I was still making Veronica happy: when she was at home I barely left her side and was rewarded with cuddles, treats and smiles.

Then, one day I was playing in Veronica's bedroom while she talked on her phone. (She talked on the phone *a lot*.) She'd just come home from an outing and had returned with lots of brightly coloured bags which were now in a pile on the bed. She often came back with these sorts of bags and I'd always wondered what was in them, so when she wandered into the bathroom, still busy with her phone, I took my chance to hop on the bed to investigate.

I had a cautious sniff, but it didn't smell like the bags contained food, which was what I'd been secretly hoping, so I jumped back down again – and honestly, that was as much investigating as I had been planning to do, but then one of the bags toppled over and a box fell out onto the floor. I glanced over at the bathroom door, but Veronica didn't appear, so I thought it wouldn't hurt to take a closer look.

Inside the box was lots of crinkly papery stuff that made a lovely rustling noise when I pulled at it, but under that was something even better: a pair of shoes.

Before I go any further, I should say that chewing is one of my favourite pastimes. My teeth are still growing and they can be a bit uncomfortable at times, but having a really good chew makes them feel much better. Veronica had given me some toys, but they were soft and squeaky: what I needed was something hard that I could really get my teeth into. Something like . . . a shoe. And these were such *interesting* shoes: they had bright red bottoms, lots of dangly straps on the front and a long, hard, sticky-out bit at the back that was just the right size and shape to fit in my jaws. It made a wonderfully satisfying crunch when I bit down on it. Well, it was so perfectly chewable that I just couldn't help myself.

Settling down in a warm patch of sunlight by the window, I spent some blissfully happy moments with the shoe; I was having such a good time, it honestly didn't even occur to me that what I was doing was wrong. I had managed to tug off some of the straps and was making excellent progress with the sticky-out bit, when suddenly—

'No, Mr Snuffles, NO!' Veronica flew across the room with a shriek that sent me scurrying under the bed, tail between my legs.

'Oh my God, no. Noooo, not the Louboutins!'

She picked up the shoe, turning it over in her hands, then spun round to where I was cowering, her eyes blazing.

'You are a bad, bad dog, Mr Snuffles. BAD DOG!' And she threw the shoe at me, catching me painfully on the leg as I fled from the room in terror.

Well, I didn't get many cuddles from Veronica after

that. From then on I was kept shut in the kitchen, where I only really saw Shirley, who I'm sorry to say never grew to love me as I hoped she would. Whatever I did made Shirley angry. She shouted at me if I trod in my bowl and spilt my food; she shouted at me if I barked at an interesting sound outside; she even shouted at me if I was having a nap on the floor because I was 'getting under her feet'. I thought that if I could only make Veronica smile like she had when I first arrived, then everything would be OK again, so whenever I saw her I'd jump up and lick her, but that just seemed to make her cross. It's no excuse, I know, but that's why I chewed up the cushions of my dog bed. I was desperate for Veronica to notice me again, to remember that I was still there. Another of my brilliant plans that ended in disaster . . .

Which brings me to today. Despite my loneliness, when Richard and Veronica put me in the car this morning the idea of running away hadn't even crossed my mind. In fact, I was excited about the prospect of visiting a new place and spending some time with Veronica (without Shirley). Over the past few days I had got a sense that change was in the air. Something called 'Christmas' was approaching – Veronica, Richard and Shirley were all talking about it – and strange things were happening. For example, a huge tree suddenly appeared *inside* our house! Odder still, it was covered in shiny silver balls and tiny lights. I hoped that whatever this Christmas thing was – if it was important enough to turn the world topsy-turvy – perhaps it could make Veronica love me again.

I was squashed up in the boot with suitcases and a large box, and from the tantalising aroma coming from within I knew it *definitely* contained food, although frustratingly I couldn't investigate further, as I was effectively boxed in. Car journeys always make me sleepy, and I'm not sure how long I'd been dozing when I was woken by Richard and Veronica talking, and it sounded like the subject was me.

'But he's such a badly behaved dog, Rich,' Veronica was saying. 'He's always jumping up and scratching me. He put a run in my Valentino silk skirt the other day.'

'He's only saying hello,' said Richard. 'Perhaps you should take him to puppy training classes? He's still so young, he just needs to be taught how to behave.'

Veronica sighed. She sounded sad, which made me feel sad too.

'I did warn you that a retriever might be a bit of a handful,' Richard went on. 'Yes, the puppies are gorgeous, but they grow into big dogs. You can't blame Mr Snuffles for playing up. He needs to be walked every day, at least once, to burn off some of that energy.'

'I'll talk to Shirley,' said Veronica.

'Darling, he's your dog,' said Richard gently. '*You* should walk him.'

'But I really don't have time.' Another sigh. 'We should have got a kitten after all.'

At these words I felt a sharp pain inside me. My worst fears had come true: Veronica didn't want me any more. With a whimper I dropped my head onto my paws, and soon the motion of the car lulled me back to sleep.

When I woke again I realised we had stopped, but looking out of the back window all I could see were rows and rows of cars, so it didn't seem like we had reached our destination.

'I'll go and get some coffee,' Richard was telling Veronica. 'Why don't you take Mr Snuffles for a quick walk to let him stretch his legs. We've still got another hour or so of driving to go.'

Grumbling about the cold, Veronica put on my lead – I was too broken-hearted to greet her with licks and a wagging tail as usual, although she didn't seem to notice – and then walked me through the rows of cars to a stretch of grass bordered by trees.

'Come on, Mr Snuffles,' she snapped. 'Hurry up and do your business, it's freezing out here . . .'

While Veronica stamped and waved her arms to keep herself warm, I bounded about in absolute ecstasy. For the first time in my life I was out in the open, on a stretch of grass uninterrupted by buildings or roads. I took a tentative sniff of the ground and felt energy coursing through me like sunlight, easing my heartache and making me want to run and jump. *This* was what I'd been missing! The lead didn't let me roam very far, but I was in raptures. The grass was alive with sounds and smells, and no sooner was I chasing one delicious scent then I was pulled in the opposite direction following some other tantalising trail. I barked with sheer happiness, which made Veronica tug sharply at my lead, and then suddenly out of the corner of my eye I spotted movement in the trees. My head snapped up and I froze, scanning the thicket – yes, there was definitely something moving there. Before I could even think about what I was doing, my instincts took over. I made a sudden bound forward, so fast that I slipped my collar, and then I was running as hard as I could. Oh my goodness, what an amazing feeling! This was what I was born to do. I could hear Veronica calling me, but I couldn't have stopped even if I'd wanted to. By the time I reached the trees whatever had been there was long gone, but I kept going, racing joyfully through the undergrowth, and I didn't stop until long after Veronica's shouts had faded away.

When I eventually came to myself, pausing by a trickle of a stream to gulp down a much-needed drink, I looked up to discover that I was surrounded on all sides by woodland. There were no people, no buildings, no roads or pavements, just trees. It was definitely time to be getting back. I stood for a moment looking around, still panting from all the exertion, trying to get my bearings so I could retrace my steps, but I hadn't really been paying any attention to where I was running – and anyway one tree really looks much like another – so I had no idea which way to go. Somewhere above me there was a sudden shriek; probably just a bird, but it was so loud in the silence that it made me jump. This was the first time in my life I had been completely alone and I was beginning to feel a bit panicky. Then I spotted a fallen trunk overgrown with ivy that I was pretty sure I remembered jumping over on the way here, so with a spring in my step I headed off in that direction. This had been a brilliant adventure, but I really should get back to Richard and Veronica.

I wandered on for a while, pausing every now and then to listen for the sound of the busy road that would signal that I was headed in the right direction, but apart from the murmur of leaves, all was eerily quiet and nothing I passed looked remotely familiar. *Don't worry,* I kept telling myself. *Soon you'll hear Veronica calling for you – maybe Richard too, because he'll be missing you as well – and they'll be so pleased to find you that you'll probably get a big cuddle and maybe a treat, and then you can curl up in the car and have a lovely sleep. Yes, everything is going to be OK . . .*

Gradually the trees thinned out and I found myself

standing on the edge of a field. Behind me were the woods, ahead of me was nothing but rutted earth, still bearing the stubbly remains of some crop, and beyond that more fields and then nothing but endless sky. I stared in wonder for a moment, stunned to discover for the first time how big the world was; the space and silence were overwhelming. Just behind me some small creature rustled in the dead leaves, but rather than chase after it I stayed where I was, staring out into the unknown. I felt a shiver of fear go through me as I realised there was no doubt about it: I was well and truly lost.

The white stuff has begun to fall again and is now settling on my fur, but it doesn't matter because at long last I've made it: I've reached the source of that delicious roast chicken smell. It's coming from a small house set on its own (rather than being squashed up next to lots of others like the ones on Richard and Veronica's street) with funny little windows and a low, sloping roof with a chimney sticking out of the top, out of which curls a trail of wood-scented smoke. I wriggle under a fence and drag myself up the garden towards the house. It takes me ages to cover the relatively short distance because the garden is on a slope and this white stuff is very slippery. It's exhausting. I get a little way up the hill only to slide back down again.

I finally make it to the house and only now do I realise just how tired I am. But I can't give up just yet; I still need to find a way to get inside. The light that I spotted from all that way off is coming from the front window. It looks like it's the kitchen. I jump up on my hind legs to get a better view and catch glimpses of a woman moving about inside, talking to someone while she tidies things away. She has shoulder-length brown hair and smiles a lot, and I get the strong sense that here is a kind and loving human. I may still be very young, but my dog-sense for such things is already keen. As tired as I am, my tail begins to wag in anticipation. I feel sure that if I could just get her attention, this woman would take pity on me and at least bring me in out of the cold for the night – perhaps even spare me some scraps of that chicken.

I bark as loudly as I can and then wait, alert for any signs that I've been heard, but there's just more silence. My legs, so weary from their long journey, are wobbling, and I collapse to the ground, shivering with cold, but I won't give up yet. I can't give up: I *have* to make her hear me. This is my only chance of rescue.

I struggle to my paws and begin barking again, but I'm so weak now that the swirling white stuff drowns out my cries and eventually my bark fades to a whimper. I can't have come all this way only to fail, surely? I've been trying so hard to stay brave, but now all hope seems to be lost . . .

Picking myself up again, I half-walk, half-crawl through the cold, searching for another way into the house. Beyond the border of the garden is a road. There are no cars, but I can tell because of the tyre tracks in the white stuff. I look around and guess that I'm near the front of the house. *Yes, here's the front door!* Perhaps I could attract the woman's attention by scratching on it? That might just work . . .

I barely notice the jolly garland of leaves and berries hanging on the door, or the silver lights covering a nearby bush, which makes the white blanket on the ground seem alive with tiny stars; my only focus now is summoning up the last of my strength to clamber onto the doorstep. I scrabble frantically at the door, convinced that someone will hear me, but nothing happens and the door stays firmly shut.

Unable to go on, I slump onto the doorstep, sapped of all energy and hope, and then everything turns black.

❄ *One Week Until Christmas* ❄

I'm jolted awake by a sudden scream from somewhere very close and am instantly on the alert for danger, but something's wrong. I can't stand up, I can't feel my paws, I can barely even see anything – just bright light and a blinding, total whiteness.

For a moment I'm gripped by panic, but then the memories of last night come rushing back, my surroundings begin to come into focus and I realise that there's a brown-haired woman looming over me. It's the same woman I saw yesterday, on whose doorstep I must have spent the night.

She is wearing a long pink dressing gown with a pair of furry boots and is staring at me with bewildered shock (I'm guessing that scream must have come from her), but I'm comforted to see that there's also genuine concern in her bright blue eyes.

The front door behind her is still open and from it radiates a blissful warmth.

She turns away and calls inside the house. 'Ben! You need to come out here and see this.'

Turning back to me, the woman bends down and holds out her hand, letting me snuffle at her fingers. They smell of toast, reminding me that I haven't had a proper meal for almost a whole day now. I try to wag my tail, to show her how happy I am to see her, but I feel so weak it's barely a flicker.

'You poor little thing, you must be freezing,' she says tenderly, brushing the white stuff off my fur, and the warming touch of her hand makes me realise just how cold I am. Then over her shoulder a man – this must be Ben – looms into view.

'Claire? What's wrong?' His eyes fall on me. 'It's a puppy!' he exclaims, astonished. 'Wherever did you find him?'

'I came out to get the milk and he was just here, lying on the doorstep. At first I thought he might be injured, but he seems OK. He's clearly very weak though; he can barely lift his head.'

Ben crouches down next to the woman – Claire, I think I heard him say her name was.

'Hello there, Puppy,' he says, stroking my head. I'm desperate to get up and greet my human saviours properly, but my legs are still numb. 'Someone must have lost him,' Ben mutters almost to himself. 'He looks like a pedigree: he's far too smart to be a stray, just look at that coat . . .'

Despite my predicament, I feel a twinge of pride and am glad that he can see beyond my muddy outer layer.

'He's not wearing a collar though,' continues Claire, picking me up and cradling me in her arms. 'Oh, he's freezing!' She cuddles me closer, and I bury my nose in the softness of her dressing gown, breathing in her scent, which reminds me of the bunches of flowers that Veronica always had around the house. 'Wherever did you come from, Puppy?'

They both gaze at me for a moment, as if waiting for me to answer, and then Ben gets up and walks down the path to the front gate.

'Maybe his owners are still nearby.' He leans over the

gate and looks up and down the lane. 'I could go out and have a look for them?'

Claire shakes her head. 'No, I think he's been on the step for a while. He was covered in snow, poor little mite.'

Snow — so that's what this white stuff is. I love learning new human words. Not bits of the moon after all, then.

'Well, I'm sure whoever he belongs to must be frantic with worry,' says Ben. 'I'll ask around the village later, see if anyone's reported a missing puppy.'

Claire nods. 'OK, but for now we need to get him warm and give him something to eat. I'm surprised he didn't freeze to death out here.'

While Ben collects the milk bottles from the doorstep Claire carries me inside, and the warmth — and prospect of food — instantly begins to revive me. As weak as I am, I take advantage of my place high up in Claire's arms to get a proper look at my new surroundings. This must be their living room: there's a huge sofa piled with cushions in all different colours, comfy armchairs, a brick fireplace, candles, framed photographs on every surface, piles of books and magazines — stuff *everywhere*.

It's hard to make out the colour of the walls because there are so many pictures hanging on them, but the low ceiling is white and criss-crossed with beams of dark wood, while beneath the jumble of brightly patterned rugs on the floor I catch glimpses of grey stone. Claire and Ben obviously don't have a Shirley to tidy up after them, which is a huge relief. In fact, this place is about as different from Richard and Veronica's echoey all-white house as you can get and feels so much more welcoming. I can well imagine making myself a nest among those sofa cushions or curling up in front of the fire. The comforting aroma of toast and coffee hangs in the air, along with the smells that I've come to associate with this Christmas thing: a pleasing spicy sweetness mingled with the fresh, sharp scent of that strange indoor tree. Sure enough, Claire and Ben have a tree too, although it's very different to Veronica's, which was far taller and decorated with silver balls and matching lights. 'Elegant' was the word she used to describe it. I don't think Veronica would be very keen on Claire and Ben's tree with its riot of rainbow-coloured decorations, glittery garlands, flashing lights and the jumble of paper-wrapped packages at its foot, but I think it looks much more exciting. It's not just the tree that's been decorated either; there are branches of holly leaves and berries above the fireplace, swags of tufty foliage up the banisters and a sprig of ivy hanging over the front door. There's so much greenery it looks almost as if the garden has decided to creep inside the house to shelter from the cold! Christmas seems an even bigger deal here than it was back in the city.

Most peculiarly of all, there is a gigantic red sock dangling from the chimney breast. Now I like socks as much as the next dog – they usually smell quite interesting and can be good for a chew – but why would you hang it on the wall? Also, and at this thought I feel a little worried, how big must the human be whose foot fits *that* particular sock? I wouldn't have thought they'd even be able to get through the door!

We've now reached the kitchen, which I saw though the window last night, and it's just as cosy as I had hoped. There's a big wooden table in the middle of the room surrounded by chairs, while at the far end is a huge pale-blue oven, which is making the whole room feel beautifully warm, and it's on a rug next to this 'Aga', as Claire calls it, that she now places me. I watch as she pours some milk into a saucepan and puts it on the hob to heat and then goes to the fridge and brings out something covered with foil. Could it be . . .? Yes, that smell is unmistakable: it's the roast chicken!

Claire puts the bowl of milk in front of me and I find the strength to struggle to my paws and begin gulping it down, spluttering as I go, desperate to get the warming liquid inside me as quickly as possible.

'Here you go, Puppy,' says Claire, holding out a bit of chicken. I swallow it whole, licking my lips to make sure I've got every scrap of that scrumptious flavour, and then nose at her leg in the hope of more.

'You're a hungry boy, aren't you?' She smiles, and a moment later to my delight she puts another bowl in front of me filled with leftover chicken – meat, scraps of skin, morsels of delicious jelly – and stands back as I wolf it down, my tail wagging in ecstatic approval.

'Looks like someone's feeling a bit better,' chuckles Ben, who has just appeared in the kitchen, putting his arm around Claire as they watch me tuck in.

I *am* feeling better – and happier than I have in as long as I can remember – which means that I can now give Claire and Ben a proper thank you, jumping up and covering them in grateful licks. Claire scoops me into her arms, giggling as I nuzzle her face, while Ben looks on in amusement.

Now that I've recovered a little I take the opportunity to have a proper look at my new human friends. Claire is probably about the same age as Veronica, but she is far less shiny and altogether softer and less angular – she certainly feels much nicer to cuddle up against. Her brown hair is piled on top of her head in a way that suggests it was done very quickly, and her face isn't painted like Veronica's always used to be. You can actually see her skin, rather than the powdery brown and pink stuff that Veronica applied every morning. Claire's obviously used to caring for others too. I can tell by the way she does thoughtful things like warming my milk. Ben is younger than Richard and messier too (his reddish-brown fur is all over the place) but in a cosy, comfortable kind of way. He smells of cut grass and wood, which is a bit odd but much nicer than Richard's strong, peppery scent. All in all, I feel very lucky that it was *their* doorstep that I ended up on, and a seed of hope plants itself inside me that I might have found a home here.

But although Claire and Ben are smiling, I can also sense that something is not quite right. They both look very tired, but it's not just that: there's a sadness in their eyes, a hollowed-out kind of look that suggests something bad has happened to them. I wonder what it could be? There is a lot of love between the two of them, that much is clear, but they have shared pain too.

You might think this is all a bit much for a young puppy to figure out, but as I grow I'm realising that I seem to have a real sensitivity to human emotions, an affinity with their innermost feelings. It was part of the reason why my final weeks at Richard and Veronica's were so distressing. I could tell, deep down, that Veronica didn't really love me any more.

Hopefully, in time I'll discover the reason for Claire and Ben's sorrow – and then, perhaps, I might be able to help them, to repay their kindnesses to me – but for now I've been hit by a fresh wave of tiredness, which is making me sway sleepily on my paws.

'He needs a bed,' says Claire. 'I'll find him something suitable.'

Deep in thought, Ben watches her moving around

the kitchen. When he eventually speaks, his voice is ever so gentle.

'You know his owners will come for him, don't you, love? A puppy like this will already have a home – and even if he doesn't, we can't keep him. Not with everything else we've got on our plate at the moment. I just don't want you getting too attached . . .'

I woof softly, desperate to convey that no, I actually *don't* have a home and I'd very much like to say here if it's not too much trouble, but his eyes are fixed on Claire.

'I know that,' she says quietly. 'But I can make him comfortable until they do.'

Moments later I'm tucked up in a small wooden crate that smells of earth and potatoes, snuggled into a nest of soft towels. I have a full tummy, I'm warm and feel safe and content, the memory of yesterday's ordeal beginning to fade with the hope that I might be able to make a home here, despite what Ben said about not being able to keep me. I very much doubt my previous owners will come looking for me: I must be miles from where I ran away, and I'm guessing Veronica won't be *that* bothered about getting me back. Even my worry that something isn't quite right in Claire and Ben's lives, that some unknown danger is threatening their happiness, is beginning to ebb away. As sleep washes over me, my mind drifts back to my extravagant bed in the city, with its pillows and lace-trimmed canopy, and I wonder how something so luxurious could be so much less comfy than a battered old potato box . . .

When I wake again it's already begun to get dark outside: I must have slept for the whole day! Yesterday's adventures must have really taken it out of me. I yawn and have a stretch and then notice that a bowl of water and some newspapers have been placed next to my bed, so I have a drink and then hop back into bed again; I'm far too comfy to get up just yet.

The kitchen is empty; I wonder where Claire and Ben are? I can hear sounds of movement from somewhere upstairs, and there's the smell of something delicious wafting from the Aga, so they're obviously not far away. I tilt my head, listening to the household noises; I can just about make out Claire's voice, but I don't think she's talking to Ben. Although it's ever so faint, the answering voice is too high and soft to be a man's. It sounds more like . . . a child! I feel a leap of excitement. Could I have been lucky enough not only to have found a wonderful new home, but a new playmate too?

Sitting up in my box, I put my nose to the air as my mum taught me. Mingled in with the smells of the house that I'm already familiar with, I now catch the trail of some other new and intriguing smells. Yes, there's definitely the trace of a human other than Claire and Ben, but also, to my surprise, I'm now strongly aware of another animal smell. It's not a dog though, I'm sure of that.

Just then I hear the front door open and Ben's voice calling for Claire as he stamps the snow off his feet. My instinct is to bound up to the front door to welcome him home, but for now I force myself to sit still. I want to be on my very best behaviour so that Ben wants me to stay. The idea of being turned out of this cosy home with nowhere to go is just too frightening to consider.

'How did it go?' I hear Claire asking him.

'Nobody in the village has heard anything about a lost puppy,' says Ben, sounding a little mystified. 'I've asked the vet to put up a notice with our details, and

I'll email the council later, but beyond that I'm not sure what else we can do.'

Nothing, I think to myself. *Do nothing. I'm very happy here, thank you very much.*

'It's strange, isn't it?' Claire replies. 'He can't have wandered that far by himself; he's obviously still very young. It's a miracle he didn't get hit by a car.'

'Well, I'm sure his owners will be in touch soon,' says Ben. 'And if not, the council will be able to take him in until a suitable home can be found.'

I feel a sharp twinge of alarm. I don't know what the council is, but I don't fancy finding out.

'Let's talk about it after supper,' says Claire as she enters the kitchen. 'Oh, hello! Look who's awake.' She bends down to pick me up, dropping a kiss on my head. 'Come on, Puppy I should think you need a loo break.'

The garden is still covered with a thick layer of snow, and now that I've regained my strength I find out just how much fun this cold, white stuff can be. I scamper around in circles, sending great clouds of it up into the air, and then discover that if I dig down I can reach the grass underneath with its multitude of interesting smells. I plough through the snow nose first, sneezing as I go, tracking the scent trails and feeling just as wildly joyful as I did yesterday when I got my first taste of freedom – although this time, when Claire calls me I return to the house straight away.

To my delight there's a bowl of food waiting in the kitchen which I bolt down, remembering not to step in my bowl or spill it on the floor, and then I jump back into my box, my tail at full wag.

'What a well-behaved puppy you are.' Claire smiles, scratching under my chin in just the right spot. 'I wonder what your name is?'

Once again I feel relieved that I no longer have my collar. I'm as pleased to see the back of Mr Snuffles as I am to have got rid of Shirley. Hopefully Claire and Ben will think of a more suitable name for me.

From my cosy spot by the Aga I watch as Claire and Ben prepare dinner. They stir pots on the stove, fill glasses and lay the table – for three people, I note with curiosity. Shirley always did these tasks at my old house, usually grumbling to herself as she did so, but Claire and Ben move about the kitchen in a much more upbeat fashion, and the smells coming from the Aga are far more tempting than anything Shirley ever produced.

Then, just as I'm about to nod off again, something *very* exciting happens. Claire disappears and when she comes back into the kitchen there's a little girl cradled in her arms. I whimper and fidget with excitement; I'm going to have a new playmate after all! But just as I'm about to leap out of my box to give her an enthusiastic welcome, something about this little girl's appearance stops me in my tracks. Far from being a boisterous ball of energy like most puppies, she is lying limply in Claire's arms, as if she doesn't even have the strength to hold her head up. I look more closely and now notice her pale skin – almost as pale as her light gold hair – and the dark circles beneath her eyes. She looks so weak, as if she hasn't eaten anything for ages. Whatever could be wrong with her?

But then she sees me. In an instant her eyes light up, she breaks into a beaming smile, and I get a glimpse of the happy little girl inside.

'Here he is,' says Claire, crouching down next to me and propping the girl up on her knee so that she can stroke me. 'Do you want to say hello?'

'Be gentle, Puppy,' warns Ben, but I don't need to be told – I can see how fragile she is. I lick her fingers and gently nudge at her legs, my tail wagging in greeting, and am thrilled to be rewarded with delighted giggles. When Claire and Ben see how happy the little girl is they exchange smiles of their own. I feel so proud to have made the whole family happy, even if it's only for a moment.

'Emily, this is Puppy,' says Claire, stroking me. 'Puppy, say hello to Emily.'

'Oh, he's like a fluffy teddy bear! Come here,' says Emily, patting her lap, so I get up on my hind legs and rest my paws on her legs, careful not to scratch. Now that I'm closer I lick her cheek, which makes her giggle even more. 'Look, he's kissing me!' she says delightedly. 'Mummy, can he stay with us for ever?'

'I'm afraid not,' says Ben, making my heart lurch with sadness. 'I'm sorry, sweetheart, Puppy's just visiting.'

'Oh Mummy, please, *please* can we keep him?'

'I'm so sorry, darling, he already has a home,' says Claire, and I feel ever so slightly encouraged by how regretful she sounds about this. 'Do you remember I told you that Puppy's lost, and we're just taking care of him until his owners come to collect him?'

Emily frowns. 'But when will they come?'

'I'm not sure. We don't know who he belongs to.'

'So they might not come at all?'

Claire seems unsure how to reply and looks over to Ben, who gives the slightest of shrugs.

'We'll see,' she says eventually.

Seemingly satisfied with this answer, Emily returns her attentions to me. 'What's his name?'

'We don't know,' answers Ben. 'What do you think his name should be?'

Emily wraps her arms around me, squashing her face into my fur. 'I'm going to call him Teddy Bear, because he's so cuddly and gorgeous. Aren't you, Teddy?'

Teddy. Ted-dy . . . I like that! Maybe Ted when I'm older. Yes, I think this new name will suit me very well indeed. I give Emily another lick and wag my tail to show how pleased I am with my new name.

'Right, supper time now; you can play with, er, Teddy a bit more later,' says Ben, scooping Emily up and seating her in her chair – and it suddenly strikes me that maybe she can't use her legs at all.

Emily's face instantly falls. 'I'm not hungry,' she says quietly.

'Just try and have a little bit, it'll help you get your strength back. It's shepherd's pie, your favourite.'

With a sigh Emily picks up her fork and takes a mouthful, to the obvious relief of her parents, although after that single forkful she just pushes the food around her plate. Whatever shepherd's pie is, it smells mouth-wateringly rich and meaty, but I can't let that distract me. I need to concentrate on the conversation to see if I can discover what's wrong with Emily.

'Did you watch your new DVD earlier?' Ben asks her.

'No.' She stares at her plate, shoulders slumped. 'Too tired.'

'We had fun reading together though, didn't we, darling?' says Claire.

But Emily just shrugs.

'Well, you've got your final hospital appointment with Dr Patterson next week,' says Claire brightly. 'I'm sure he'll have some good news for us.'

To my dismay, Emily suddenly looks as though she might cry.

'Mummy no, I don't want to go back to that hospital. Please don't make me!'

'Darling, I'm sorry, but we need to see Dr Patterson again – he has to check how you're doing. It won't take long, and we might see that lovely nurse Rosie again. Remember the one who gave you those nice sweets?'

But Emily is shaking her head. 'No. I'm not going.'

'Please Emily, it's important that we get you checked over.' Claire's voice is trembling and she seems close to tears herself. 'You have to remember that you were very, very poorly, sweetheart. At one point we thought you might even—'

'Claire.' Ben shoots her a warning look and she drops her head, taking a breath to steady herself. I'm almost shaking myself; it sounds as though Emily has been terribly ill – no wonder Claire and Ben are so anxious.

Emily turns to Ben. 'But I haven't got men-in . . . men-in-gitis any more, have I, Daddy?'

'No, but—'

'Then why aren't I feeling better?' She looks imploringly between Claire and Ben. 'And why do I get so tired?'

'You will be better soon, my darling, I promise,' Ben tells her gently. 'But it'll take a little while for you to be able to run around like you used to. Meningitis is a nasty disease and you were very poorly, as Mummy said. We just have to be patient and trust Dr Patterson.'

From where I'm sitting in my box I see Claire reach for her daughter's hand and give it a tender squeeze. 'The hospital appointment won't take long, Ems. I promise. Dr Patterson just needs to make sure that you're still making good progress, OK? After all, you need to be on top form for when Father Christmas comes next week!'

At this Emily brightens up a little. 'Do you think he'll bring me a bike?'

'I'm absolutely sure of it,' says Claire. 'You asked for one in your letter to him, didn't you? And you have been a very, *very* good girl this year.'

Emily now breaks into a broad grin. 'I have, haven't I?'

'Yes, sweetheart, you have,' says Ben, returning her smile.

Emily thinks for a little while. 'Well OK, I suppose I *could* go and see Dr Patterson again, as long as he promises to be very quick.'

'I'm sure he will be,' says Claire, relief flooding her face.

'And as long as Nurse Rosie gives me some sweets.'

'Consider it done.' Ben smiles.

'And as long as Teddy can stay with us for ever,' finishes Emily firmly.

At this her parents exchange anxious glances. I hold my breath, waiting for their answer . . .

'Well, even if Teddy can't stay with us for ever, I'm sure he'll be able to visit us a lot,' says Claire eventually. 'Now, how about you try another mouthful of that shepherd's pie?'

After they have finished supper, Emily comes to sit on the kitchen floor so she can play with me. I'm relieved to see that her legs do work, but she's very weak. Claire finds a ball in one of the kitchen drawers and rolls it across the floor, which sends me scampering happily after it, making Emily giggle and clap. I retrieve it in my jaws and then – resisting the strong urge to take it back to my box for a good chew – trot back to Claire and drop it at her feet, to the obvious delight of the whole family.

'What a good boy you are, Teddy,' exclaims Claire, patting my head. 'Your owners must have trained you very well.'

Hmmm, I'm not sure Veronica would agree with that, I think, remembering her appalled face after I chewed her shoe – and my bed, and her handbag . . . But things are different now; I desperately want to be on my very best behaviour, not only so Claire and Ben are happy for me to stay, but because making this lovely family smile, after everything they have been through with Emily's illness, is such a wonderful reward.

'Right, bath time for you, missy,' says Ben, dropping a kiss on his daughter's head.

'Nooooo, not yet. *Please*, Daddy! I want to play with Teddy a bit more.'

Her dad frowns. 'I don't think so, Emily. It's getting late . . .'

'I've got an idea,' says Claire. 'Why don't we give Teddy a bath first? I'm not sure what adventures he got up to before he arrived, but he is rather grubby, aren't you, little one?'

She smiles at me and I wag my tail, but inside all I'm thinking is, *Uh-oh*.

As I've said before, I'm rather proud of my coat, which was the whitest and fluffiest of all the litter. I had quite a lot of compliments about it while I lived with Veronica and Richard, and my fur certainly doesn't look its best after being covered with mud during my journey here. But I'm really not keen on baths. At all.

Admittedly, I've only had one, but that was enough to last a lifetime. Even now the memory of it makes me shudder: the overpowering sickly smell of the bubbly stuff that Veronica rubbed in my fur, how angry she got when I gave my coat a good shake and – worst of all – that noisy, buzzy thing that she used to blast hot air at me when shaking would have been a *far* more effective method of getting dry. No, all things considered I will happily live with a less-than-dazzling coat if it means never having to have a bath again. But Emily seems so excited about the idea, and Ben mutters something about how I 'won't be allowed in the bedrooms until I've had a wash', so it seems I have no choice.

All too soon Ben is carrying me upstairs to the bathroom, where Claire has run some water into the tub and prepared a pile of towels. It is far cosier than Veronica's cavernous marble bathroom and, like the living room downstairs, is crammed full of stuff. There is a clutter of plastic toys along the bath's edge, magazines piled up by the loo and bottles lined up on the window ledge. Emily is sitting by the side of the bath, looking almost as happy as she did when talk turned to Christmas, and the room is wonderfully warm. Still, a bath is a bath. Every fibre of my being is telling me to run away NOW, but I need to be brave. Besides, if I can survive a night on a freezing-cold doorstep, then surely I can survive a bath. Can't I . . .?

'Right, Teddy, are you ready?' asks Claire. Before I can somehow convey to her that no, I am most definitely not ready, in fact I most likely never will be, she picks me up and plonks me in the water. Well, at least it's warm – but that's the only thing this bath has got going for it. I stand absolutely still, hoping to keep my contact with the water to an absolute minimum, but the wetness quickly seeps through my fur until I'm soaked to the skin. *Ugh, this is just as bad as I remember.* Humans often confuse me, but the biggest mystery of all must be why they seem to enjoy taking baths so much.

I try to tolerate the water for a while longer, but it's no good. It's just too unpleasant; I need to get out *now*. Before Claire can stop me, I launch myself at the side of the bath, trying to jump out, scrabbling to get a foothold, but it's too high and slippery and I end up falling back and getting water everywhere – even in my eyes, which I have to say is extremely unpleasant, and I can't even rub them with my paws because then I'd fall over and end up getting even wetter.

'It's OK, Teddy. Just stand still and let Mummy wash you,' says Emily. 'It's not so bad, I promise.'

Resigned to my waterlogged fate, I realise I have no choice but to stand here and wait for the ordeal to be over. I glance up at Claire, a glum look on my face.

'Aw, poor Teddy,' she says with a sympathetic smile. 'Not a fan of baths, then? I'll be as quick as I can. Here, why don't you have a chew on this?'

She produces the ball we were playing with earlier, which makes me a little less miserable, and after a while I begin to get used to the sensation of the water. As long as I don't have to have any of those nasty, smelly bubbles on my fur this might – *might* – be OK.

'Right, Teddy, I'll just put on some shampoo to get off the mud,' says Claire, and to my horror she produces a bottle of green gloop, pours a dollop into her hands, works it into a mound of bubbles and then rubs them into my coat.

I shut my eyes and screw up my nose, waiting for

that offensive smell to hit me, but after a few moments I realise that although there is a bit of a scent it's very faint and not that unpleasant, and Claire is washing my coat so gently that it's actually just like having a nice, if rather damp, cuddle – plus Emily's delighted expression as she watches makes it easy to cope with the less-than-pleasant bits, such as getting my face washed. As Claire pours cupfuls of warm water over me, rubbing away at the matted bits of my coat, it's a relief to feel the clumps of dirt being washed away. That mud was making me itch. Yes, I reckon I might have to reconsider my hard line on baths, although I've certainly not changed my mind about those horrible bubbles. I'm chewing away at the ball and am actually beginning to enjoy myself when, before I can think what I'm doing, I give myself a vigorous nose-to-tail shake to get rid of some of the water.

For a moment there's chaos: Claire and Emily are screaming, I'm desperately scrabbling to get out of the bath to escape the noise, sending more water flying around the bathroom, and Ben rushes in to find out what's happening. At the sight of his shocked expression, I freeze in horror. Oh no, what have I done? I brace myself, waiting for the angry shouts that I have no doubt will come.

But then, to my astonished relief, I realise that Claire and Emily, although both now drenched, are laughing – and now Ben is too. He wraps Emily in a towel and gives one to Claire, then lifts me out of the bath and puts a towel around me too. Overjoyed that by some miracle he doesn't seem to be cross with me, I cover his face with a flurry of grateful licks.

'It's OK, Teddy, I think I'm quite clean enough already,' says Ben, but the tenderness in his voice makes me feel more certain than ever that I have found my for-ever home.

Later that evening I'm curled up in my box by the Aga, listening to Claire and Ben chatting as they tidy up the kitchen. The moon is shining through the window and I realise that it must have been about this time yesterday that I was on the other side of that window, desperately hoping that someone would notice me; I really couldn't have imagined then how wonderfully well things would turn out for me. I stretch, sighing with contentment. I can't believe how lucky I have been to have stumbled across such a loving family.

Emily has had her bath and is now asleep, and from what I can gather from her parents' conversation she was cheerier at bedtime than she has been in a long time.

'She's so excited about Christmas, bless her,' Ben is saying. 'It's great that she's got something to look forward to.'

'Yes, but you know that's not the only reason Emily's happy tonight, don't you?' says Claire.

They both look over to my bed, and I put on my cutest sleepy puppy face.

'You know we can't keep him, love,' says Ben gently. 'Even if we wanted to – and I'm really not sure we could cope with a puppy on top of everything else right now – it's only a matter of time before someone comes to claim him. Of course Emily loves Teddy, he's adorable, but he's not ours.'

Claire sighs; she looks so sad. I wish I could tell them how desperate I am to be part of their family, as I can't imagine ever finding a cosier home or more caring owners. I think back to earlier this evening when all three of them were laughing while watching me play with the ball. In those few minutes Emily's illness was all but forgotten and she was like any other little girl, happy and carefree, while her parents' eyes sparkled with joy. It's such a lovely feeling, knowing that I made them all so happy, even if it was just for a moment, and I resolve to try my hardest to make them smile like that again tomorrow – and hopefully the next day, and the day after that . . .

Then a thought pops into my mind that makes my tummy flip with excitement and my ears prick up. Maybe finding my way to their doorstep wasn't just luck? After all, it's very strange I ended up here, goodness knows how many miles away from my first home, in this particular house. Perhaps – and I know this sounds a little strange – perhaps I was *meant* to find this family. Maybe I was somehow brought here to them?

With that, suddenly everything is clear to me. I didn't end up here because of what Claire, Ben and Emily can do for me, but because of what I can do for *them*. I am here for a reason: to heal this family's heartache and help them smile again. I have a purpose. And because of that I'm absolutely sure, despite what Ben says, that I'll be staying.

❄ *Six Days Until Christmas* ❄

Good morning, world; you're looking very beautiful today!

I'm snoozing in my cosy potato-box bed with the sun streaming through the window, gently warming my fur. The sky is beautifully blue and cloudless, and it looks like the snow is beginning to disappear. In a way I'm sorry to see it go as it was such fun to play in, but at least it means I can now have a proper explore outside and find out what's under those mysterious snow-shrouded lumps and bumps in the garden. First things first though: now that I'm feeling better and am back to my usual bouncy self, I need to have a proper explore *inside* my new home.

I can hear movement upstairs and what sounds like water running. There's nobody in the kitchen, so after a quick sniff under the table, which yields a few tasty crumbs, and a peek through a door that's been left slightly ajar (which – oh my goodness! – seems to be some sort of walk-in food cupboard . . . although I am certainly not going to risk getting in trouble by investigating further), I trot into the living room. At first glance it seems to be empty too, so I decide to begin with a closer look at that Christmas tree. Then I realise Emily is lying on the sofa under a blanket. Her eyes are closed; I wonder if she's asleep?

Moving as quietly as possible so as not to disturb her, I pad across the room to check on her. I know she needs to rest, but if she's awake then I would love a cuddle. We might even be able to play a game – a very gentle one, of course. Like any puppy, I know I can get a bit overexcited at times, but I'm discovering that I have a real nurturing instinct towards Emily. I feel a need to care for her and keep her safe. It's funny really: all this time I've been hoping for a new mum, but now I'm acting like one myself! I'm thrilled that as I approach her Emily opens her eyes and, on seeing me, breaks into a huge smile.

'Teddy!' She reaches her hand down to me and I nuzzle her fingers, my tail wagging furiously. 'How are you this morning? Come up here with me so we can talk.'

She pats the sofa and, once I've jumped up next to her, pulls herself up into a seated position. I'm relieved to see that she seems stronger than she was yesterday and she has more colour in her cheeks too.

Emily presses her face into the ruff of thick fur around my neck. 'You smell very nice after your bath, Teddy. Like Haribo sweets.' She glances over to the staircase and then drops her voice to a whisper. 'Mummy and Daddy say you can't live with us because you already have a home, but I think you should stay here. Would you like that?' I lick her cheek to show her that yes, I would love that, and she giggles. 'Hey, that tickles! When I'm better I'll take you out for walks every day and we can have races round the garden. I like running. I used to do a lot of running before I got sick. And skipping and swimming and climbing.' Emily suddenly looks sad. 'I was in hospital for a really long time, Teddy. Like, for *weeks*. I really don't want to go back there again.' She sighs. 'Oh, it wasn't too awful, I suppose. Dr Patterson and the nurses were nice, but I couldn't *do* anything. I just had to lie there in the same boring room feeling yucky while everybody else was doing stuff and having fun. Do you know what I mean, Teddy?'

In a way, I know exactly what you mean, I think, remembering how I felt when I was shut away at Richard and Veronica's, desperate to get outside.

'I haven't been to school for ages,' Emily goes on. 'Before I got ill I used to make a fuss every morning about going to school, but now I really, *really* want to go back. I miss my friends the most, but I also miss the lessons. I even miss the teachers – except for Mrs Williams.' Emily pulls an expression like she's eaten something nasty. 'Mrs Williams is a hundred years old and has a face like an angry raisin and she shouts at us the *whole time*,' she whispers, with another grimace. 'Anyway, when I first got ill my friends used to come and visit me a lot, but I couldn't really play with them because I had to stay in bed, so they got bored, and now they don't come so much any more.' She rests her head on me. 'I get a bit lonely sometimes . . . But I've got you now. You're my friend, aren't you, Teddy?'

We sit on the sofa together for a while; Emily talks about herself and introduces me to her cuddly penguin, Cyril – 'My second-best friend, after you of course, Teddy' – and I try to show that I'm listening by giving her lots of licks and nuzzles.

And then Emily asks me, 'Can you do any tricks, Teddy?'

I look at her with my head on one side, unsure what she means.

'OK, first of all, get on the floor,' she says, giving me a gentle shove off the sofa. 'Now, Teddy, sit!'

Ah, so that's what she means by doing tricks. Veronica used to tell me to 'Sit' the whole time and got cross when I didn't, but I really couldn't understand why it seemed so important to her. I still don't understand, really. Perhaps it's a game? I stay standing and wait to see what Emily asks me to do next, but she begins to tell me to do lots of other complicated things like 'Shake hands' and 'Do a dance,' and I'm afraid I don't have a clue what she expects of me, although thank-fully Emily doesn't seem to mind too much when I just stand there wagging my tail. She pats her lap again and I jump back up.

'Shall I tell you a secret?' Then she lifts up my ear, and whispers, 'I think Father Christmas brought you here as an early Christmas present.'

Ah, this mysterious Christmas thing again.

'You see,' Emily goes on, 'I've been secretly wishing for a puppy for ages now, and then you suddenly arrive on the doorstep! Mummy and Daddy think you're lost, but I know you're meant to stay with us, because Father Christmas brought you.' She gives me another cuddle. 'You're probably too young to know about Christmas, aren't you, Teddy? Well, it's this special day when Father Christmas brings you presents and everyone eats too much and sings songs about the Baby Jesus.'

Well, no wonder everyone is so excited. Food, parties, presents – Christmas is even better than I thought! I have no idea who this Jesus is though – perhaps he's Father Christmas's baby? I wonder if I'll get a present too?

'*That's* where Father Christmas will put my presents when he comes on Christmas Eve,' Emily is saying, pointing to the giant sock hanging from the fireplace I'd spotted yesterday. 'But between you and me,' she goes on conspiratorially, 'I'm a bit worried because I've asked him for a bike, and there's no way a bike will fit inside that stocking. Mummy says not to worry, that Father Christmas will work it out because he knows magic, but I'm not so sure . . .'

She yawns and rubs her eyes. I should probably leave her to have a rest, but I'm so comfy that I snuggle up with her, and within a few moments the rise and fall of her chest starts to slow and soon I can tell she's fallen asleep.

Wide awake and a bit bored now that Emily isn't talking to me, I decide that it's time to have an exploratory sniff of that Christmas tree. To my surprise, as well as the distinctive tree smell I get the whiff of something edible – something sugary and delicious. I quickly track down its source to some of the decorations. These particular ones are white with red stripes and shaped like little sticks. Wow, they smell amazing! I wonder if Claire and Ben would mind if I tried one? Emily did say that Christmas was about presents and eating – and they *are* just hanging on the tree as if they're sort of . . . asking to be eaten.

Before I have second thoughts, I use my paw to bat one of the sweet-scented decorations off the branch and take a bite: it makes a satisfying crunch. Oh, that is incredible! The clear plastic stuff around the outside isn't very nice, so I spit that out, but the stick itself is sugary and extremely tasty indeed.

I intend to stop at one, but it is so delicious – and I haven't yet had anything to eat this morning – so I have another and another, until I've gobbled up all the decorations I can reach, feeling very Christmassy as I do so. At least Claire and Ben won't have to worry about giving me breakfast *now*!

Right, where to explore next? I've snuffled my way around the kitchen and living room, and there aren't any other rooms downstairs, so I guess the only way is up. I can go and say good morning to Claire and Ben. I'm sure they won't mind if I come upstairs – well, they haven't told me I'm not allowed up there.

I still find stairs a bit of a challenge, so I hop up one at a time, keeping my eyes fixed firmly on my paws so I don't slip. I'm concentrating so hard that I don't notice that the strange animal scent I was aware of last night is getting stronger until I reach the top of the stairs and come face to face with a large tabby cat sitting on the landing.

For a moment I freeze in surprise, but then I quickly remember my manners and trot towards her, tail wagging, to introduce myself. How wonderful, another playmate! My first ever owners had a lovely moggie called Nelly, who was good friends with my mum, and although I know that cat-and-dog relations can sometimes be a little tricky (Mum told us about this) Nelly was always very gentle with us puppies. At times she even let us cuddle up with her. But just as I reach this new cat, intending to give her a friendly snuffle of greeting, she swipes me hard across the nose with her paw. *Ouch!* I back off whimpering, wondering what on earth I've done wrong.

The cat stays where she is, staring at me through slightly narrowed yellow-green eyes. She's a big cat – bigger than me – and I really don't want to get off on the wrong paw, especially if we're going to be family. Perhaps I *was* being a little too boisterous.

I decide to make another attempt at a greeting, and this time I approach her very politely and slowly with my eyes on the ground, to let her know that I'm being respectful to her as an elder, but as soon as I get within swiping distance of her she does it again, and this time it really hurts. With both my pride – and nose – injured, I'm about to make a rapid retreat downstairs when suddenly the cat turns tail and bolts off down the corridor. I finally work out what's happening – she wants to play! Silly me, sometimes I can be so slow to catch on . . . With a woof of excitement, I bound after her, chasing her into the bathroom, where she jumps up onto the window ledge, knocking the bottles and jars that were lined up there clattering onto the floor. Wheee, this is fun! I keep barking to tell her how much I'm enjoying our game, and it's obvious that she is too because she keeps running along the window ledge – in fact, she seems to be going faster than ever now – and then she leaps off, dashes out of the bathroom and down the corridor into another room. Wow, she's really very good at this game; I can barely keep up with her! Hot on her tail, I realise from the stacks of toys and the dolls on the bed that we're now in Emily's bedroom. The cat leaps onto the desk, scattering paper, books and crayons all over the pink carpet, then scuttles up the side of the wardrobe in that amazing way that cats can, finally coming to rest at the top.

I sit at the bottom of the wardrobe, my tail wagging happily, and look up at my new friend to see if that's the end of the game. To my alarm, however, she doesn't actually look like she's enjoyed herself very much. I'm no expert on cat emotions, but I would describe her expression as absolutely furious. Her tail is flicking from side to side and she is staring at me through angrily slitted eyes.

Hmm . . . it appears that I might have misread the situation after all. Perhaps she wasn't wanting to play when she ran away, perhaps she was just . . . running away.

'What the hell is going on?' Ben bursts in, his dressing gown flapping about his bare legs, and I watch anxiously as he looks around the room taking in the mess, the infuriated cat on top of the cupboard and me, trying my hardest to look innocent. He reaches up to stroke the cat, his face a picture of concern.

'Shhh, Martha,' he says gently. 'It's OK, Puss, you're safe now . . .' She meows and pushes his hand affectionately with her head. Well, she can obviously be nice if she wants to – I wonder why she was so unfriendly to me?

Ben strokes her under the chin, muttering soothing

words to her, but when he turns to me his face is altogether less kind.

'Teddy, that was very naughty!' He picks me up roughly and holds me out in front of him, staring crossly at me. 'You mustn't chase Martha. Bad boy!'

As Ben carries me out of the room I notice Martha shoot me a look that clearly says, *You lose, Dog.*

Oh dear, I can tell it's not going to be quite so easy to win over this particular member of the family. For now though I've got far more pressing worries, such as the fact that Ben is obviously very angry with me – possibly even angry enough to throw me out of the house? As he carries me downstairs, panic sweeps over me. This is meant to be my home, I'm absolutely sure of it, and the idea that Claire and Ben might not want me to stay because of this little misunderstanding with the cat is utterly terrifying.

But worse is yet to come. When we get to the living room, Ben's eyes fall on the shreds of plastic wrapping underneath the Christmas tree. There's a sharp intake of breath and I suddenly feel deeply ashamed. Why did I eat those decorations? I'm only a guest here, of course I shouldn't just help myself!

'Claire!' calls Ben, his voice tense with annoyance. 'Could you come down here? We need to talk.'

Moments later Claire comes downstairs. 'Ben? What's wrong?' She spots me and smiles. 'Good morning, Teddy,' she says tenderly, and although my tail wags in reply I hang my head in disgrace. I can't bear the idea that she might be cross with me too.

'Look at what that dog's done,' says Ben, pointing to the plastic stuff I spat out under the tree.

'What's happened, Daddy?' asks Emily, who has woken up.

'Teddy's eaten all the candy canes off the tree.'

Claire looks at the mess, and I hold my breath, readying myself for another telling-off. 'He's only a puppy, Ben,' she says, and I'm amazed to hear that her voice is still kind. 'We really should have moved them out of his reach. He wasn't to know that he's not meant to eat them.'

'He chased Martha too,' says Ben. 'I found her on top of Emily's cupboard. She looked terrified, poor thing.'

'Well, you show me a dog that doesn't chase cats. And besides, as much as I love dear old Martha, she can be quite a bad-tempered puss at times.'

'Martha scratched me once,' Emily pipes up.

'Yes, I know, darling,' says Ben patiently. 'But Martha's quite an old lady now, and Teddy can be very boisterous. Perhaps we should keep him shut in the kitchen until we can make other arrangements.'

Ben puts me on the floor, and I slink over to Claire, my tail hanging remorsefully, hoping that she'll forgive me. I know I'm in deep trouble, but I'm clinging onto the hope that there's been no mention of getting rid of me – yet.

'I've just had a reply from my email to the council about him,' says Ben, turning to Claire again. 'They haven't heard anything about a lost dog fitting Teddy's description, which is strange. A pedigree puppy – you'd think his owners would be desperate to find him, wouldn't you? The council say they have space for him in their kennels for now, and, if nobody comes to claim him they'll either look to rehome him, or else, well, he'll have to be . . .' He stops mid-sentence, glancing at Emily. *I'll have to be what?!* A dart of fear shoots through me, and I cower next to Claire.

'Surely it wouldn't come to that, Ben?' mutters Claire. Seeing her horrified expression, I begin to whimper.

What on earth is going to happen to me? Just when I thought I had found my perfect home, it looks like I'm going to be sent away, and who knows where I'll end up?

'Mummy?' Now Emily sounds upset too. 'What's going to happen to Teddy?'

Ben crosses over and sits with her on the sofa, hugging her. 'Shhh, don't you worry, sweetheart. A dog like Teddy will have no problem at all finding a new home.'

'But he doesn't *need* a new home – he can stay with us! Daddy, you said that he had to go because his owners were coming to collect him, but if they're not coming then why can't he stay here? *Please!*'

'I'm afraid it's not that simple, Emily. Teddy won't stay this size for ever; he's going to grow up to be a big dog and I'm not sure we can cope with looking after him even at the moment. I'm stuck at work all day and Mummy's very busy caring for you, so we don't have time to train him or make sure he has enough exercise. And what would we do with him when we go on holiday? I tell you what: once you're feeling better we can talk about getting you a pet. A rabbit, perhaps?'

'I don't want another pet, I want Teddy!'

Ben looks upset. I can tell he doesn't want to disappoint Emily but he's clearly made up his mind about me going. Oh, this is so frustrating! I *know* that I can help this family. I've seen how much happier Claire and Ben seemed to be when they were watching Emily play with me last night. It was as if all their worries were forgotten. OK, it was only for a moment or two, but I'm sure that given time I could make a real difference to their lives. I look over to Claire, who seems lost in thought. I might be completely wrong, but I get the feeling that she wants me to stay, and I desperately hope that she's able to persuade Ben too – unless, of course, my naughtiness today has caused a change of heart?

I can feel my heart racing with fear until finally Claire breaks the silence.

'Goodness, look at the time! Ems, you must to starving. What would you like for breakfast?'

Emily immediately brightens. 'Can I have toast with Nutella?'

'What's the magic word?' asks Claire.

'Can I *please* have toast with Nutella?'

Claire smiles. 'As it's the weekend, yes, you can. Ben, do you want to come and give me a hand?'

She looks at him very deliberately and he nods, and

they disappear into the kitchen together. Um . . . hello? What about me? How can they think about food when my whole future hangs in the balance? But when I creep over to the doorway I discover that rather than making toast, Claire and Ben are deep in conversation.

'I know that it's not a great time for us to be thinking about getting a pet,' Claire is saying, 'but are you sure we shouldn't consider keeping Teddy if he doesn't have a home? You've seen how happy he makes Emily. She hasn't smiled like that in weeks.'

'Claire, we've never even discussed the possibility of getting a dog before. It's crazy to consider taking on another big responsibility when Emily still needs full-time care. I agree that a dog might be good for her in the long term, but don't you think it would be more sensible to wait until she's recovered, then do some research into appropriate breeds?'

'Maybe, but Teddy's here *now*. He needs a home, and you've got to agree he's a lovely puppy. I know he's a bit frisky, but he'll grow out of that.'

Ben sighs and runs a hand through his hair. 'I don't know, Claire,' he says, shaking his head. 'Retrievers are a lot of work. He'll need walking every day.'

'Well, that won't be so hard, will it? I'd be very happy to take him out first thing, and you're always saying you need to do more exercise . . .' She gives him a teasing look. 'As for training him, you know my family had dogs when I was growing up, so I could certainly take care of that, and I'm sure Emily would love to help. Besides, I get the feeling Teddy's a fast learner.'

I'm so engrossed in their conversation – and so desperate for Claire to persuade Ben to let me stay – that before I can stop myself I give a little woof of agreement. They immediately look round to where I'm standing in the doorway. *Oops, I'm supposed to be keeping quiet!* But to my relief, Ben's face softens into a smile.

'Well, it looks like someone else has strong opinions on the subject,' he says. He regards me for a moment, as if making up his mind, then turns back to Claire. 'OK, Teddy can stay. For now.'

Yes! Claire beams at me, and I feel like I could burst with happiness. I *knew* this was meant to be.

'Thank you, love,' she says, wrapping her arms around him. 'I promise you won't regret it. I think it'll be good for all of us.'

He smiles, dropping a kiss on her head. 'I do have some conditions though,' he says. 'We keep him on a trial basis.'

'Fair enough,' says Claire.

'If he causes trouble he'll have to go.'

'OK . . .'

'And that includes chasing Martha.'

Claire hesitates for a moment. 'He *is* still a very young puppy, Ben,' she says. 'I think he's trying his hardest to behave, but I don't think we can expect him to be perfect.'

Ben looks over to me again, and I sit up very straight and wag my tail in a way that hopefully gives the impression that chasing cats is absolutely the very last thing on my mind. One thing's for sure: from now on I will have to be on my best behaviour. No more taking things without asking, no jumping up and *definitely* no playing with Martha.

'Well, let's see how it goes,' says Ben eventually. 'But if it isn't working out by Christmas then he'll have to go to the council kennels in the New Year.'

*   *   *

I don't want to boast, but for the rest of the day I am the model of perfect puppy-dom: I come at once when I'm called, I don't step in my food, I even manage to stop myself chasing or barking at a squirrel in the garden – and it's *so* tempting, because it keeps running up and down a tree near where I'm playing, almost as if it's taunting me. Emily is overjoyed when her parents tell her that I'll be staying (for now, anyway), and I might be imagining it but she really does seem to have more energy than yesterday. I wonder if this could be because of me? Her face certainly lights up whenever she sees me, which makes it much easier to be on my best behaviour even when that pesky squirrel reappears and stands in front of me, twitching its tail, almost like it *knows* I can't chase it. Ben is at home today as it's the weekend – apparently he'll be back at work tomorrow – and I make myself as useful as I can so that he doesn't regret his decision to let me stay. For instance, when he's shovelling what's left of the snow off the garden path I try to help by digging at it with my paws, sending a shower of wet clumps onto the heap he's already made.

'Thank you, Teddy,' he says, surprised, and I woof with pride.

Throughout the day I pay close attention to the family's conversations so I can find out more about my new owners' lives. I discover that their house has a name rather than a number like the ones in the city – it's called Glebe Cottage – and that their surname is Woods, which I like because it reminds me of trees and fresh air and because Teddy Woods has a very nice ring to it. I learn that Emily is six years old and will be turning seven in a few months' time, and that apparently birthdays are just as exciting as Christmas, possibly (judging by Emily's reaction) even more so. And, usefully, I also find out that Martha's favourite spot to nap is at the top of the stairs, when I overhear Claire and Ben discussing whether it would be better to move her basket 'up out of Teddy's reach'.

But although I feel incredibly fortunate to have ended up in such a wonderful home, at the back of my mind is the constant fear that if do something naughty Ben will send me away – and sometimes I don't even *know* if what I'm doing is naughty or not. For example, I found a ball in the living room earlier and was giving it a good chew – because I know from yesterday's game that I'm allowed to chew balls – when Claire spotted me and took it away. 'Oops, not Ben's tennis ball,' she muttered quietly. Thankfully she didn't mention it to Ben, but the point is that I'm still finding the human world and all its strange rules extremely confusing.

I have another fear too, tucked deep inside me – that one day Richard and Veronica will track me down and turn up to claim me. I know it's unlikely, but the prospect of going back to their cold white house fills me with dread.

It's a fear that comes back to haunt me that evening. Claire and Ben have finished tidying up the kitchen and are locking up the house before bed. I'd been half-hoping, now that I'm an almost-official member of the family, that I might be allowed to sleep upstairs – or at least in the living room – but Ben makes it clear that I'm expected to remain in the kitchen.

'You stay there, Teddy,' he says, turning out the light. 'Sleep tight.'

As I've said before, it's wonderfully warm and cosy in my box next to the Aga, but now that I've fully recovered from my snowy ordeal I find myself desperate to be near the family, not stuck down here on my own. It reminds me all too vividly of being shut in the kitchen at Richard and Veronica's house for hours on end with only Shirley for company – and the more I think about how sad and lonely that made me feel, the more panicky I become. I can't go back there, I really couldn't bear it . . . Since arriving at the Woods' house I've discovered that I have such a capacity for love, both giving and receiving, that the idea of living with people who don't really want me, and certainly don't need me, is too awful to even think about.

I snuggle my nose into the towels lining my bed, hoping the scent – which reminds me of Claire – will soothe me, but at this moment it just seems to amplify my loneliness. Suddenly my determination to be on my best behaviour is swept away by an irresistible urge to seek comfort.

I wait until the house has fallen silent and then creep out of my box, through the kitchen and into the living room – stopping to admire the twinkling lights on the tree as I pass – and then softly, slowly make my way upstairs. I pause on the top step to check whether Martha is standing guard; her scent is in the air, but her basket is empty and I'm pretty sure I saw her slip outside into the garden when Ben was locking up earlier.

Feeling slightly more confident now, I trot onto the landing and get my bearings. It's not quite so dark up here, as the bathroom light has been left on, and I quickly identify Emily's door at the end of the corridor.

I creep past the bathroom and another door – Claire and Ben's bedroom, I guess – and I'm nearly at Emily's room when suddenly something flies out of the shadows, quicker than a flash, missing my nose by just a whisker. *Martha!*

Somehow battling the overwhelming urge to bark or give chase, I scamper on until I reach Emily's door, my heart pounding. I glance back to see Martha's yellow eyes staring at me from out of the darkness and feel a shiver of fear. I need that cuddle more than ever now . . .

But after all that effort Emily's door is shut. I sit with my head on one side, listening hopefully, but all is quiet except for the sound of her breathing. I wonder if I should scratch on the door to try to get her attention, but it's obvious that Emily's asleep. Besides, I really don't want to risk waking up her parents. I'm reluctant to run the gauntlet of Martha again, so I curl up upside her door with a soft whimper, and it's only after I finally hear Martha padding downstairs and going out through her cat flap that I retrace my steps back to my box in the kitchen. Exhausted by my adventure, I quickly fall asleep, but my dreams are haunted by visions of cold white rooms and half-chewed designer shoes.

❄ *Five Days Until Christmas* ❄

It was still dark when Ben left the house this morning. I was woken by the front door closing, and then listened to the crunch of his feet on the gravel path and the sound of him getting into the car and driving off. I'm not sure where he was going – to an office perhaps, like Richard used to? Whatever that is, it doesn't seem like either of them like it very much. Once he had gone, the house fell silent again, save for the usual soft creaks and clanks (I get the impression it's a very old cottage, and it sometimes seems to talk to itself). Claire and Emily were obviously still asleep.

As there was no reason for me to get up just yet, I lay in my bed, watching as the sky turned from dark grey to purple to cloudy white, wondering what the day would have in store. The kitchen was as toasty as ever, thanks to the warmth from the Aga, and I felt completely content. When I lived at Richard and Veronica's I woke up every morning desperately hoping that today would be the day I finally got to explore the outside world, but now I don't really have any desire to venture further than the bottom of Glebe Cottage's garden. In fact, the thought of being out in the world on my own is no longer exciting, but actually a bit scary. I feel like I've found my home here, and it's such a lovely warm, safe sensation, just like when I was a very young puppy snuggled up with Mum and my brothers and sisters. If only there wasn't still this uncertainty over whether I can stay. Well, at least Ben will be out of the house today, which means that I don't have to be *quite* so careful not to get up to any accidental naughtiness . . .

'It's only five days until Christmas, so we've got a busy time ahead,' says Claire brightly as she tidies away the breakfast things. She still looks pale and tired, but there's a spark in her eyes and I get the impression that she's just as excited about Christmas as her daughter.

Emily, who is still in her pyjamas, is sitting at the kitchen table taking occasional bites of toast, while I hover at her feet ready to hoover up the crumbs.

'Mummy, tell Teddy what we're doing today!' she says.

'Today we have to do a very important job. After breakfast we're going to make the Christmas gingerbread cookies.'

'And you and me are going to help, Teddy,' says Emily. 'And that means we get to *lick the bowl*.'

Claire smiles at her daughter. 'Maybe you should take care of the bowl-licking by yourself, Ems. I'm not sure puppies like gingerbread very much.'

I'm pretty sure that I *would* like gingerbread, whatever it is, but that's OK. It's not as if I do badly for food here – quite the opposite, in fact. I had this amazing stuff called scrambled eggs for breakfast this morning, which is probably my new favourite thing to eat – apart from roast chicken, of course. And the cheese that Ben gave me after I helped him clear the path was very tasty too. *And* the leftovers of shepherd's pie that I had for supper last night. And . . . well, let's just say everything has been delicious.

'OK, Teddy can help me stir the mixture, then,' says Emily.

Claire nods. 'I think that sounds like an excellent job for him.'

Emily waits until her mum's back is turned and then leans down to me and says quietly, 'Don't worry. I'll give you a little taste when Mummy's not looking.'

I wag my tail with glee, which makes her grin.

Emily sits back up again. 'And what are we doing tomorrow?'

Claire's smile falters just for a moment, but she quickly recovers. 'Tomorrow,' she says brightly, 'we've got your hospital appointment with Dr Patterson.'

Emily pulls a face and folds her arms stubbornly.

'Come on, darling. You know I promised you it wouldn't take long,' says Claire.

'And the sweets,' says Emily firmly. 'Don't forget about the sweets.'

'Absolutely. I'm sure Nurse Rosie will be bringing in an especially big bag just for you.'

After a pause Emily nods as if satisfied. 'And what's happening the day *after* tomorrow, Mummy?'

'The day after tomorrow we're going to be doing a big food shop so we're ready for Christmas dinner,' says Claire.

Emily grins broadly. 'We do eat a *lot* of food at Christmas, Teddy.'

'I seem to remember that someone did last year, that's for sure,' says her mum fondly.

'Well, it was just all so yummy,' says Emily. 'Apart from the Christmas pudding. And the sprouts.' She bends down towards me again and drops her voice to a whisper. 'Don't *ever* eat sprouts, Teddy. Not even if your parents tell you that they'll make you sparkle. They don't make you sparkle and they taste like YUCK.'

I notice Claire, who has obviously overheard, trying to stifle a laugh.

'And the day after that, Mummy?' asks Emily. 'What's happening then?'

'The day after that is Christmas Eve. And the day after that . . .' Both of them finish the sentence together: 'Is Christmas Day!'

Emily squeals with delight, clapping her hands, and

I give a little woof and scamper around the table three times to show how excited I am too.

'Right,' says Claire. 'Before we start on the cookies, Teddy needs to go outside and you, missy, need to get dressed.'

'OK.' Emily climbs off her chair and makes her way towards the door. Her progress is still quite slow. It's almost possible to forget that she's ill when she's sitting down, but when you see how much effort it takes for her to walk it's obvious how weak she still is. I look at Claire, who is watching her daughter with fear and helplessness in her eyes.

'Do you want a hand up the stairs, love?' she asks anxiously.

Emily shakes her head, fiercely concentrating on each step, and in a funny way I'm reminded of myself when I was younger. I remember being so determined to be independent, to be the first of our litter to walk, to eat proper food, to try new things. Although I never had the challenges she's having to face, Emily and I are really quite similar in that way: both strong-willed, both determined and, right now, both in real need of each other.

*   *   *

After breakfast Claire lets me out for my morning tour of the garden. It's a big space, surrounded on all sides by a fence and divided up by what Ben referred to the other day as flower beds. ('Teddy, try not to walk over the flower beds, you'll trample on my spring bulbs', is what he actually said.) There are no flowers in the flower beds at the moment, but perhaps that's because it's too chilly for things to grow – I certainly wouldn't fancy living out here in the cold. The lawn slopes gently down towards a wood, in front of which there is a slide and swing, which I'm sure must have been well used by Emily before she got ill, although now they have an abandoned look about them, with patches of lichen in places. As I pass the edge of the wood I keep an eye out for that squirrel. I definitely plan to show it who's boss next time it appears, but it's obviously off tormenting some other poor dog. My guard-dog duties fulfilled, I'm about to return to the cottage when near the end of the fence I see a narrow gap between the slats. Hmmm, I haven't noticed that before . . .

Intrigued, I put my eye to the chink and get a glimpse of the garden next door. From the little I can see, it looks rather more overgrown than this one. The grass is long and unkempt and there is a great tangle of brambles and fallen-off branches heaped up at the bottom of it, over which ivy has wrapped itself like ribbons decorating a Christmas present. As I nudge my nose against the gap, trying to get a better look, I realise that the space in the fence is getting wider. I'm sure if I pushed hard enough I could probably squeeze all the way through . . .

I can't see the next-door cottage from here, but I wonder if the people who live there would mind if I had a little look around their garden? I get the impression there would be lots to explore, and there's an extremely exciting smell coming from it making my tail quiver with anticipation. I hesitate for a moment, focusing all my senses to try to get the lie of the land. It seems so quiet, perhaps there isn't actually anyone living there?

Deciding that the coast is clear, I wriggle through the gap and immediately put my nose to the ground, happily ploughing through the thick, wet grass on the trail of that scent. It only takes me a moment to know what that smell is: dog! And it's so strong that I'm sure there must have been one here very recently. I stop in my tracks and excitedly scan the garden for further proof of four-legged activity. How amazing it would be to have another dog living right next door!

The cottage that the garden belongs to is smaller than the Woods' and seems to be all on one level, rather than having an upstairs and downstairs. It isn't as pretty as Glebe Cottage either, just a squat grey box, and has the same unloved air as its garden. It's not exactly welcoming, but encouraged by the prospect of finding a new friend I trot up towards the house, passing a broken chair, moss-covered paving and what looks like the crumbling remains of a stone wall, until I get close enough to look in the large back window. There is a man inside, sitting by himself at a table eating breakfast. I'm not good at working out human ages, but I can tell he is fairly old because he has tufts of white hair on his head, and his movements are stiff and slow. My immediate impression is that this man doesn't have much happiness in his life; I can't imagine him breaking into a smile, let alone laughter. More than anything, he looks like he needs a friend.

In fact, he looks so lonely that I feel sure I must be mistaken and there isn't a dog living here after all, despite that telltale smell being stronger than ever up here, because I can't imagine a human would ever look this forlorn if he had a dog to keep him company.

Just then the man looks up and spots me through the window. Right, here's my chance to introduce myself! I give a friendly bark and wag my tail to show that I'm pleased to meet him; hopefully he'll be so glad of the company that he won't mind about me coming into his garden uninvited. At once the man struggles up from his chair and hobbles over to the window, which he then throws open.

'Oi, you! Get out of it!' he yells, waving his arms at me. He is gruff-voiced, and his face is all crumpled like a piece of paper that's been angrily scrunched up. 'This is private property! Shoo!'

I'm so stunned by this reaction that for a moment I stand there, but then the man reaches down to pick something up, and before I realise what's happening he throws it at me as hard as he can, hitting me on the leg.

Well, that gets me moving all right! I barely have time to register that the missile was a saucepan lid before I turn and dash back down the garden as fast as I can with my tail between my legs, squeezing through the gap in the fence and not stopping until I reach the safety of Glebe Cottage. Thankfully the back door is ajar, and I bolt inside and wriggle under one of the armchairs, my heart thumping frantically. I stay hidden there for a while, wondering what just happened. I'm usually quite good at working out emotions when it comes to humans, but not in this case. That man clearly didn't want a friend – either that or he doesn't like dogs. Whatever the reason, I had better steer well clear of him in future.

When I wander back into the kitchen, preparations for cookie-making are in full swing. Emily is sitting at the table, propped up on a pile of cushions with a brightly coloured sort of dress tied over her clothes, while Claire keeps disappearing into the walk-in food cupboard and re-emerging with interesting-looking – and -smelling – jars and packets.

'Right, so we've got the flour, sugar, syrup, butter . . .' Claire surveys the table, eyes narrowed in deliberation. 'What are we missing, Chef?'

'Ginger!' shouts Emily immediately.

'Of course, silly me. We can't make gingerbread without ginger, can we?'

Claire goes back to the larder and when she emerges she's carrying a small white tub. It doesn't look particularly interesting, so I settle down on the rug by the Aga and I'm licking my leg, which is still smarting from where the saucepan lid hit it, when suddenly I get a waft of something that's like nothing I've ever smelled before. It's such an intoxicating, potent scent that it's sort of thrilling and terrifying all at once. I look up, intrigued, to discover that Claire has opened the small white tub and is sprinkling a spoonful of whatever was inside into a bowl. That must be the ginger. Well, if Christmas comes with smells like this, it must be even more exciting than I've been imagining.

The radio is playing loudly, and every song that comes on seems to be about Christmas. Claire and Emily sing along, and it's such a jolly atmosphere that I join in too, howling along with the high notes, which makes them both laugh.

'Look, Teddy, it's snowing,' says Emily as Claire sifts clouds of white powder into a bowl. I sniff at it, trying to work out if it smells tasty too, but it goes up my nose and brings on a fit of sneezes. *Phew, stay away from that stuff!* Making cookies seems like quite a complicated process: Claire keeps checking in a big book then measuring and adding all sorts of things to the bowl.

'Can I stir the mixture now, please, Mummy?'

After one final look in the book, Claire hands her daughter a big wooden spoon (which I must say looks temptingly chewable) and Emily gets to work, her tongue stuck out in concentration.

'Careful you don't spill any of it,' says Claire, holding the bowl to help her, and I hop up on my hind legs to get a better look at what's going on up on the table. Not only have I got my eye on that spoon, whatever is inside the bowl smells very yummy indeed.

'Teddy has to have a go too, remember,' says Emily.

So Claire lifts me up and holds me next to the bowl. At first I'm unclear what's expected of me, but when Emily holds out the wooden spoon – 'Here you go, Teddy, your turn' – I can't believe my luck, grabbing the handle between my jaws and having a good chew, much to Emily's delight. The other end of the spoon is coated in the gingerbread mixture and my vigorous gnawing sends clumps of it flying off, splattering over Claire and Emily.

'OK, I think Teddy has done enough stirring now,' says Claire hurriedly, taking back the spoon and putting me on the floor again, and although I hadn't quite finished, I don't really mind because I feel very proud for having helped prepare for Christmas. Hopefully now Claire might let me have a little taste of that delicious-smelling mixture too.

Then suddenly I spot a movement on the window ledge and I look over to see that Martha is sitting up there, her tail wrapped neatly around her paws. *I wonder how long she's been there for?* I've been so engrossed with the cookie-making that I hadn't even noticed her come in, although she does have this unsettling ability to appear and vanish without a sound.

'Do you want to help too, Martha?' asks Emily, and I woof to invite her to join in the fun, hoping that I might be able to mend our relationship after its stormy start. By way of an answer, Martha averts her eyes and begins to wash a paw, but at least she doesn't run away. Eager for Claire to see how polite I'm being towards Martha – and encouraged by the fact that the cat continues to stay put – I cautiously make my way over to where she's sitting and gaze up at her, my tail wagging in a way that hopefully shows I'm sorry for chasing her the other day. After all, if Martha and I can get on I'm sure that would go a long way towards persuading Ben to let me be a permanent member of the family. Martha pauses mid-lick and looks down at me, her expression giving little away. I woof politely, figuring that as I'm not within swiping distance the worst she can do is run away, but she just continues to stare. Hmmm, she's not making this very easy for me . . . I suppose it was too much to hope that she might purr in reply or jump down for a nuzzle, but on the bright side I do seem to get the impression that she doesn't object to me *quite* as violently as she did before. Perhaps she's coming round to the idea of me joining the family after all? I woof again. This time she ignores me and focuses her attention back on the table, but she still hasn't tried to swipe me, so I'll take that as progress.

Claire, who has been watching us, laughs at Martha's haughty expression.

'Don't worry, Teddy. Martha doesn't really have much patience with anyone,' she says. 'She's quite an old girl now and likes to be left alone. Don't you, Puss?'

Martha's eyes glitter knowingly as if in agreement.

'She won't even sit on my knee for a stroke, Teddy,' says Emily. 'And I give the best cuddles.'

Well, that just seems strange. Emily must be the sweetest, gentlest little girl around – I can't think of anything I enjoy more than snuggling up with her. I look up at Martha again and with a jolt of surprise discover she's now looking at me, and this time her eyes almost seem friendly. Well I never! Perhaps I've been too quick to judge her; maybe she doesn't dislike me after all, she just prefers her own company. Yes, now I come to think about it, I *do* remember Mum telling us that cats tend to be more independent than dogs, and if Martha is quite elderly, then a bouncy puppy and a playful little girl probably aren't her ideal companions. I resolve to keep making an effort with her, but to keep a respectful distance – for now, at least.

'Teddy, come over here.' I look round to see Emily crouched on the floor, beckoning me over, holding something out towards me. 'Quick, before Mum comes back in again.'

Intrigued, I scamper over and discover that Emily is holding out a dollop of something sticky and sweet-smelling. I gobble it down and lick her fingers, making sure I get every last sugary scrap, my tail wagging in appreciation. Contrary to what Claire thought, puppies *do* like gingerbread – very much, in fact!

Emily beams at me. 'It's yummy, isn't it?' She runs her finger around the bowl and offers it to me again. 'Here you go, have a bit more . . .'

I hesitate for a moment; I'm not sure if this counts as being naughty and I really don't want to get in trouble, but Claire is still out of the room and the gingerbread mixture really is very delicious, so I go in for another taste and then, to show how much I enjoyed it, cover Emily's face with grateful licks.

'Hey, stop it, Teddy,' she squeals. 'You're making me soggy!' But she pulls me closer to her, giggling all the while, which just makes me lick her even more.

'You're my best friend, Teddy,' says Emily, burrowing her face in my fur. 'Promise me you'll never leave us.'

I give her a nuzzle in reply, and then I notice that Claire is standing in the doorway, watching us. I might be mistaken, but it looks like she has tears in her eyes.

*   *   *

The morning's excitement has taken its toll on Emily, who goes for a lie-down on the sofa and quickly falls asleep, so I trot back to the kitchen to keep Claire company while she tidies up. Martha has vanished just as silently as she appeared. The gingerbread is now in the oven, filling the house with its warm aroma and making it feel more Christmassy than ever. I curl up in my bed and rest my head on my paws, watching Claire as she works.

'It's so lovely to see Emily playing with you, Teddy. I haven't seen her laugh like that since before she got ill,' she says, taking an armful of ingredients back into the larder. 'These past few months have really taken it out of her, poor little thing. The old Emily would have been chasing you round the house non-stop – I don't think you'd have been able to keep up with her.' Claire smiles to herself. 'Before the meningitis she was always on the go: skipping, cycling, roller-skating, climbing trees . . . She was the most fun-loving, adventurous child you could imagine. But then overnight all that energy, all her joy and spirit, just . . . disappeared.'

I sit up in my bed, ears pricked up to show Claire that I'm listening. She seems to want to talk about her daughter, and I'm keen to find out more about what happened to Emily.

'Anyway, since you arrived I've seen glimpses of the old Emily, and it's given me hope that one day, given time, she'll make a full recovery and we'll get our happy, wild little girl back again. The doctors are being careful not to let us get our hopes up – they have to, I know, it would irresponsible to do anything else – but every time we go to the hospital they seem to feel the need to remind us how seriously ill Emily was, how lucky she is to be alive . . .' She trails off, shaking her head. 'Don't they think we know that already? To see your child lying in a hospital bed, covered in tubes, wired up to machines. To wonder if she's going to pull through . . .' Claire stops what she's doing and leans heavily against the sink. 'I think about that every single minute of every day,' she says softly.

She stays like that for a while, then wipes her eyes, takes a deep breath and goes on. 'So yes, of course I know how lucky Emily is to be alive, but if she can pull through that – if she can beat the odds – then who's to say she can't make a full recovery, eventually?'

Claire looks over to me, a beseeching look in her

eyes, and although I know she's not really asking me –
and is certainly not expecting an answer – I want her
to know that I'm quite sure that Emily will get better,
because I can sense just how strong her spirit is, so I
wag my tail and give a woof of reassurance.

Claire laughs in surprise.

'What an amazing dog you are,' she says. 'It's almost
as if you understand what I'm saying.' Then she laughs
to herself, shaking her head. 'I really am going mad.
Well, even if you don't, Teddy, you're a very good listener and it really does helps to talk about it, so thank
you.'

Claire dabs her eyes again and gets back to work,
piling the dirty crockery into the dishwasher, but after
a little while she begins to talk again.

'These last few months have changed me too, Teddy,'
she says. 'I used to be . . . what's the right word? Com-
placent, I suppose. Everything in my life was going
so well. I had a wonderful husband, a perfect child, a
good job – I felt almost untouchable, as if bad things
only happened to other unfortunate people. And then
suddenly – *bam*. One moment everything is great, the
next I'm in intensive care with doctors telling me that

my daughter might not survive the night.' Her back is to me now, and I see her shoulders slump. 'Something like that has got to change you. I'm sure it makes some people appreciate every moment and live life to its fullest, but for me the opposite happened. I sort of . . . lost my faith in life. I stopped trusting that everything would turn out OK, because I'd seen how quickly it could all be snatched away. And then I lost my job, on top of everything else . . .' She trails off into silence again and I'm left wondering how this poor family has made it through and how desperate I am to make life better for them. 'I used to be quite a positive person, but now I wake up every morning feeling, well, feeling scared. Sometimes the future just seems so bleak.' Claire hesitates for a moment, as if lost in her thoughts, then turns to face me. 'Sorry, Teddy. You don't want to listen to me wittering on, do you?

I trot over and gently nudge her knee with my nose to show her that I'm actually very happy to listen to her, and to my relief she breaks into a smile.

'Oh you do, do you?' She crouches down to scratch behind my ears and immediately seems less careworn. 'And now you're here, making everyone smile again.

Who would have thought it? Turning up on our door-step like a little lost orphan.'

Enjoying the attention, I roll over so she can tickle my tummy.

'Who do you belong to, Teddy? Emily loves having you here, and I can see how good you are for her. But what if your owners do turn up, hmm?' She shakes her head at the thought. 'That would be awful. I worry it would be worse for Emily if she gets attached to you and then you get taken away. Maybe Ben's right, and we should send you off to the council for rehoming . . .'

Oh no, that's a simply terrible *idea!* I jump up from the floor and put my paw on her leg, my head cocked to one side, trying to communicate how much I want to stay.

She smiles at me again. 'Oh don't worry, little one. I'm far too soft to do that. And it's not just Emily who likes having you here, you know, I'm quite happy about it too. And he might seem a bit grumpy sometimes, but I know Ben does as well. Just don't go chasing Martha or chewing anything you're not supposed to, OK? Ben's pretty stressed right now – not just with Emily, but also this situation at work . . .' Again she tails off and I wonder what's going on. Is there some other problem the family are dealing with? I decide I need to find out more, so I can help them. And then, almost if she's reading my mind, Claire says, 'The best thing you can do now is not to get into any trouble, OK?'

❄ *Four Days Until Christmas* ❄

Goodness, is it the morning already? I'm so tired it feels like the middle of the night. But here's Ben padding around the kitchen in his slippers making tea, and the man on the radio is talking about breakfast, so I guess it must be time to start the day.

I have a stretch and a shake to try to wake myself up. Like most puppies I do like to sleep, and I had a bit of a late bedtime last night because Ben didn't get home until long after Emily had gone to bed. When he finally appeared, the first things I noticed were his bleak expression and the grey shadows under his eyes. He looked like he had a lot on his mind. Claire, who was in her dressing gown by this time, reheated his supper – she'd eaten by herself a few hours before – and they sat at the kitchen table together talking until long after the time humans are usually awake. I kept drifting off, but I was trying my best to keep track of their conversation as their worried expressions and the lack of laughter suggested they were discussing something important. Sure enough, they kept mentioning money, something I've noticed that humans can be quite preoccupied with. Veronica and Richard certainly talked about it a lot too, although their conversations were usually prompted by Veronica spending too much of it (I remember one such chat after the shoe-chewing incident), whereas Claire and Ben seemed concerned they didn't have enough of it. Although I didn't really understand what they were saying – Ben kept mentioning things called 'debts' and 'loans' – they looked quite upset. I thought it best to stay in my bed and not intrude, but when the conversation turned to Emily's hospital appointment – at which point Claire began to cry – well, that certainly got me up pretty quickly! I hopped out of bed and went straight over and put my paws on her knees to try to comfort her, and was rewarded with a smile and a stroke. Then Claire lifted me up on her lap, where I curled up and fell fast asleep while they carried on talking. I don't even remember her putting me back into bed.

'Morning, Teddy. Do you want to go out?'

I jump out of my box to greet Ben, tail wagging enthusiastically – a little *too* enthusiastically as it happens, as I'm suddenly hit by the urge to yawn and I trip over my tail, ending up in a heap at his feet. Whoops.

'Looks like someone could do with a few hours' more sleep.' Ben grins, giving my head a friendly ruffle. 'You and me both, mate.'

I follow him to the front door and he lets me out into the garden.

'Those lazy girls are still in bed,' he says. 'I'm going to let them sleep for a little while longer; we've got a big day ahead.'

As he shuts the door behind me, I stick my nose up in the chill air to find out what's going on. I think this is possibly my favourite time of the day: early in the morning when the world is waking up and tantalising traces of the night's adventures still hang in the air.

Weirdly, the garden seems to be covered in a cloud this morning – I can barely make out the woodland beyond the fence – and the grass has turned white and stiff overnight, making a funny crunching sound when I walk on it. I wonder what this could be – something to do with Christmas, perhaps?

Within moments the fresh air works its magic, flooding me with energy and sending me scampering around the garden in circles, and then suddenly I see it. *The squirrel.* He's sitting on the top of the fence not far from me, motionless apart from an occasional twitch of his bushy tail. We stare at each other for a moment, then to my astonishment the squirrel hops down and begins making its way across the grass towards me in such a bold fashion that it's almost as if he's taunting me.

Well, I'm afraid it's just too tempting. Before I can think about what I'm doing, my instincts kick in and I set off at full pelt towards the squirrel, barking up a storm – 'This is MY garden, squirrel, clear off!' – making it scuttle up the nearest tree, where it perches on a branch just out of reach and peers down at me. The cheek of it! I keep barking at the top of my voice, trying to scare it off, and I'm so engrossed in my guard-dog activities that I don't notice Ben running down the garden, waving his arms, until he's almost on top of me.

'Teddy, NO!' His voice is a shouty whisper. 'Be quiet! It's not even seven o'clock. You'll wake the whole neighbourhood!'

On seeing Ben's infuriated expression – the same expression he had on discovering Martha on top of the wardrobe the other day – I freeze. *Oh no, what have I done?* All I had to do was behave myself, and now here I am, back in trouble again – and on today of all days, when the whole family is worried about Emily's hospital appointment. Not only that, but I'd completely forgotten about the angry old man next door! I can't imagine he's going to be too happy about being woken up this early. Oh my goodness, what happens if he comes round? I flinch at the memory of his furious face and the pain of being hit by that saucepan lid. Crouching down, my tail between my legs, I hang my head in fear and shame.

Then I hear Ben sigh. 'It's OK, Teddy. I know it's fun chasing squirrels, but it's far too early to be making so much noise, OK?'

I glance up, encouraged by the gentleness in Ben's voice, and to my astonishment he doesn't look cross any more. Could this mean I'm forgiven?

'Come on, let's get you back inside,' he says, setting off up the garden, and I follow him, giddy with relief. 'You'll have to stay at home while we take Emily to the hospital, so I'll take you out for a walk after breakfast to work off some of that energy. I can give you a tour of the neighbourhood, OK?'

I perk up immediately. A walk? Now that does sound interesting. As much as I'm content with my limited horizons at Glebe Cottage, it'll be nice to see a bit more of the village and get my bearings. I might even meet some other dogs!

Due to my unexpected arrival, the Woods family don't have any of the usual doggy things (hence my potato-box bed and water bowl emblazoned with the word puss), which means that I don't have a collar or lead either. So when Ben suggests taking me for a walk, Claire, as resourceful as ever, quickly makes me a harness out of a length of red ribbon.

When it's ready, she looks at me and says, 'Teddy, sit!'

Oh my goodness, what is it with humans and this 'Sit'

thing? Surely it would be easier to put the harness on me while I'm still standing? It doesn't make any sense at all.

'Sit!' says Claire again.

This is so confusing! Unless . . . perhaps 'Sit' doesn't mean sit after all, and has some completely different meaning in this context that I'm as yet unaware of? All things considered, it seems much more sensible to stay standing, which is what I do. With a slight huff of frustration, Claire bends down and ties on the harness (and, as I thought, it goes on far more easily than if I had been sitting).

'There you go, practical *and* Christmassy.' She smiles, stepping back to admire her handiwork.

Ben nods his approval and then pulls Claire in for a kiss. 'You clever old thing,' he says softly, looking at her with such tenderness it makes my heart give a little hop of happiness.

'Hey, not so much of the "old", thank you,' says Claire, breaking into a grin and putting her hand gently on Ben's cheek. It's wonderful to see how much love there is between them, despite all their worries.

Although the harness isn't particularly uncomfortable, I'm really not keen on being on a lead. It brings back unpleasant memories of being tied to a café table, bored and frustrated, while Veronica chats to her friends. Ben and I have barely made it down the garden path when I realise that I could escape from my new harness with very little effort. After this morning's incident, however, I'm desperate not to upset him again, so I trot obediently by his side, only pulling a tiny bit when a cat jumps off a wall right in front of us and surprises us both.

'Good boy, Teddy,' says Ben approvingly, and I hold my head high, proud that I'm managing to keep my instincts in check and not chase after every tempting scent that I get wind of. I can't wait to get out to explore my new surroundings. I just hope that pesky squirrel doesn't make a sudden appearance . . .

The lane outside Glebe Cottage winds gently down a hill, on one side of which there are a few other cottages, most of which have wisps of smoke curling from their chimneys, and on the opposite side nothing but woodland and fields. A few of the trees are still a brilliant green like our Christmas tree, but many have lost their leaves and are now bare-branched but for a scattering of birds perched on their spiky silhouettes. The early-morning cloud has now cleared away, leaving the sky a brilliant blue, while the cold air is crisp and sweet-smelling, with the occasional pleasing waft of sweet woodsmoke. It's the sort of day that's made for being outside. The birds obviously think so too, as they keep up a constant chattering and whistling as we stroll along the lane. In the city the hum of traffic was constant, day and night, but here only the occasional car passes us – which makes it even more of a shock when a huge vehicle with wheels that almost reach up to Ben's head rumbles down the narrow lane towards us. I cower behind him, terrified, as it roars slowly by, so close that it almost brushes my whiskers; there are no pavements here.

'That's a tractor, Teddy,' he says, looking at me quizzically and giving me a reassuring stroke. 'So you're not a country boy, then?'

Hmmm. I really don't fancy getting up close with one of those things again. Thankfully the road we now turn into is slightly wider and has a pavement, which makes me feel a bit less exposed. It passes over a river, and Ben stops for a moment on the humped bridge, giving me a chance to inspect some interesting-looking birds floating in a cluster by the reeds.

'No chasing the ducks, OK?' says Ben as I hop my front paws onto the railings to get a better look, my tail wagging furiously. 'I really don't fancy fishing you out of the river.'

The surroundings are getting more built-up now – although compared to the city it's still very quiet – and there are more people here too, bustling in and out of shops. I can almost smell their excitement and anticipation; it seems that everyone is busy getting ready for Christmas. One shop in particular looks popular, with a queue of people snaking out the door and along the pavement, and as we get closer I discover why. Displayed in the window is every variety of meat you could possibly imagine: sausages, chickens, steaks, hams . . . The smell alone is making my mouth water uncontrollably, and it's taking every last ounce of self-control not to slip my harness and make a run for it. Whenever Veronica took me shopping it was to buy clothes or shoes, but this is *my* kind of shop.

I don't know whether to be relieved or disappointed when we pass the meat shop without going in (actually I do: relieved, as I'm not sure I would have been able to trust myself in such close contact with all those gorgeous-smelling goodies), but I distract myself from dreams of sausages by admiring the cheerful Christmas decorations hanging in every window and over every door. There is even an enormous light-covered tree with a star on the top sitting in the middle of the village green. It's such a pretty sight, and I find myself hoping that Emily has been able to come down and see it.

We are now walking towards a large building that stands a little distance apart from its neighbours. It looks very old, like Glebe Cottage, but is much bigger and grander, with rows of windows and a sign hanging over the door with a picture of one of those huge animals with horns that I crossed paths with on the day of my great escape. I feel Ben pick up speed, as if he's keen to get past this place as quickly as possible, but just as we hurry past the front door a woman steps out and sees him.

'Ben! Long time no see!' She looks delighted to see him. Ben looks less happy.

'Oh hello, Diane. How are you?'

'All good, thank you,' she says with a smile. 'Well, busy. You know how crazy things get at Christmas: we're fully booked across the whole period. No rest for the wicked though, eh?' She looks down at me. 'And who's this young chap then?'

'Long story. His name's Teddy.'

The woman bends down and gives me a stroke, smiling at me. 'Well aren't you a gorgeous little thing? I bet Emily loves you!' She glances up at Ben. 'How's she doing?'

'Not too bad. We've got another hospital appointment today, so we'll see what the doctor says.'

'Well, I hope it goes really well,' she says, still stroking me. 'And how's Claire holding up?'

'She's fine.' Ben's voice is tense.

Neither of them speaks for a little while. There's a sort of awkwardness between them, I can tell. Then the woman stands up to face him, an apologetic look on her face. 'Ben, I'm so sorry about what happened.'

'It's OK,' he says shortly. 'Really not your fault.'

'I know, but when we found out how badly the management had treated Claire – that they were letting her go just for missing a couple of weeks' work because of Emily's illness . . . Well, we all felt terrible for her.' She shakes her head as if in disbelief. 'I reckon she could sue them for unfair dismissal, you know. She was a bloody brilliant head receptionist, the best I've ever worked with. Everyone loved her.'

'Honestly Diane, it's fine. And in a way it's probably better that Claire can be at home to look after Emily.'

He smiles, but it's plain to me that he wants to get going. The woman, however, doesn't seem to notice.

'And how's your new business getting on?' she asks brightly. 'Claire told me you were setting up your own garden design firm. She was so proud of you! Must be nice being your own boss, eh?'

Ben shifts uncomfortably. 'I've had to put the garden business plans on hold for a little while – just until Emily's back on her feet and Claire finds another job. So I'm still working where I was before, in insurance.'

'Ah, right.' The woman looks a little embarrassed. I might not understand everything that's being said, but their emotions couldn't be more obvious. 'Well, I'm sure you'll get your business started before long,' she goes on. 'Let me know when you do; our garden could definitely do with a makeover!'

Ben plasters on a smile that doesn't reach his eyes. There's another uneasy silence. 'Well,' he says, 'we better be getting on . . .'

'Of course. Give Claire my love, won't you? We do miss her.'

'Sure. Have a great Christmas.'

As we walk away quickly, I look up at Ben questioningly.

'That was where Claire used to work,' he tells me once we've walked on a bit. 'The Bull Hotel. Diane and the staff are nice enough, but let's just say the manager's not my favourite person right now.'

We walk on in silence, Ben clearly wrapped up in his thoughts. His whole body is tense, like he's about to break into a run, and at one point he kicks a stone across the ground so hard it makes me flinch.

'Oh, I'm sorry, Teddy,' he says, immediately apologetic. 'Don't mind me. It's just been a difficult few months, what with Emily's illness and . . . other worries.' And with that, he falls frustratingly silent again. Unlike Claire, he's not much of a talker. I wish he would open up a bit more; I might be able to help.

On the way back we take a different route across the fields, avoiding the High Street and the Bull Hotel, and I get a glimmer of hope that Ben will let me off the lead now that we're away from the road. I catch wind of an interesting scent and can't stop myself pulling, but Ben doesn't take the hint or perhaps he's worried I might run off. Never mind, it's just wonderful to be able to explore the outside world knowing that I've got a lovely home to go back to. My tail is wagging furiously and I'm literally skipping across the stony furrows of the field in delight.

As Ben watches me he breaks into a smile. 'I feel the same way as you, Ted.' He laughs. 'I just love being out in the open air. It's not much fun being stuck in an office day in, day out, I can tell you. Anyway, now I'm on holiday, and having a week away from *that* place is about the best Christmas present I could get.' He suddenly grimaces, and I wonder what this 'office' thing is. It doesn't sound like much fun, and Richard didn't seem to like spending time there either.

'Oh I shouldn't complain,' Ben continues. 'I know I'm lucky to have a good job, but it's difficult to be passionate about life insurance. I don't suppose you know what insurance is, do you, Teddy?' He glances down at me, and I give a little woof just to let him know that I'm listening, and he breaks into an astonished smile. 'Oh you do, do you? Well then, you'll appreciate it's not what I dreamed of spending my life doing. And I was *so* close to setting up my own business.' Ben gives a huff of disappointment. 'Claire and I had talked about it for years and we had it all planned out: Woods Garden Design. Sounds pretty good, right? We'd done the numbers, bought the tools, taken out a lease on a van, and everything was ready to go – we even had a couple of clients lined up – then the week before I was going to resign from my insurance job, the Bull Hotel gave Claire her marching orders. Eight years of faithful service and they sack her for taking time off to be with Emily in hospital.' He shakes his head in disgust. 'So, the gardening business has been put on hold for now. I know I can make a success of it, but it would be slow at the start, so we'd need Claire's salary to support us.' Ben bends down, picks up a stone and throws it into the distance, staring after it long after it lands. When he speaks again, it's as if he's talking to himself. 'I don't know. Maybe I should just forget the garden business, knuckle down and make the most of the career I've got, rather than chasing dreams. After all, the most important thing is that I can take care of Claire and Emily.'

As I watch Ben, clearly absorbed in his thoughts,

I feel like I might understand him a little better. I can sympathise with him wanting to take care of his family; that's certainly the way I feel towards the Woods too, and I'm sure my desire to protect them will only become stronger when I'm a grown-up dog. But at the same time I know what it's like to have dreams and to want something desperately. It's hard to put those feelings to one side, even if you know it's probably the right thing to do . . .

Dragging his attention back to the present, Ben looks at his watch. 'Ah, we'd better get going. We don't want to be late for Emily's appointment.' He bends down and rubs me under my chin in just the right spot. 'Thanks for listening, buddy.'

We are making our way up the hill towards Glebe Cottage when a man appears and starts down the hill towards us. A shiver of fear goes through me as I realise it's the man from the cottage next door, but my terror at seeing him again after yesterday's painful encounter is quickly tempered by my excitement at seeing that he's not alone: trotting along by his heels is a white and tan spaniel. I *knew* I could smell dog there! I just hope that the spaniel is a little friendlier than its owner.

Interestingly, Ben seems just as unenthusiastic as I am about the prospect of meeting the man from next door.

I hear him groan softly. 'Oh God, this is all I need . . .' As we get nearer though he plasters on a smile and says brightly, 'Morning, Tobias. All well?'

The man gestures towards me with a grunt. 'This *your* animal, then? I caught him sneaking about in my garden yesterday, making a terrible mess of my lawn, and I suppose it was him making that infernal racket at the crack of dawn this morning?'

I feel myself bristling at the man's accusation – his garden was already a mess; it was absolutely nothing to do with me! – but my indignation quickly vanishes because I'm so entranced by his dog. She's the most beautiful animal I have ever seen: her silky coat falls in tumbling curls around her ears and haunches, while her long-lashed eyes are bright with warmth and intelligence. I suddenly feel sure we're going to be great friends.

'Hello, I'm Teddy,' I tell her a little shyly. (I'm *so* glad I don't have to introduce myself as Mr Snuffles.)

'It's a pleasure to meet you, Teddy. I'm Lady.' She's

not on a lead, so she comes over to me and touches my nose in greeting. She has such a lovely, elegant manner, I find myself hoping I don't do anything to embarrass myself. 'Have you just moved to the area?' she asks politely.

'Yes, I have. I'm staying with the Woods family.'

'I think I heard you this morning. Let me guess – was it the squirrel?'

'Yes!'

'I thought it must be,' she says. 'That animal likes nothing better than winding up dogs. My human, Tobias, lives in the cottage next to yours, so that means we're going to be neighbours.'

I wonder whether I should mention my explorations in her garden yesterday but decide it might be better to wait until I know her better. She might think I'm impolite, and I'm desperate to make a good impression on her. Who would have thought that grumpy old Tobias would have such a sweet-natured dog? I briefly think about asking Lady if she would like to play right here and now, but she seems far too serene to be a rough-and-tumble type of dog. Tobias and Ben are deep in conversation (I'm not really concentrating, but it seems to be something about fixing a fence) so when she sits down, I sit too, thrilled to have the opportunity to speak further.

'So, Teddy, where were you living before this?' she asks, her head to one side.

'In a city, a long way away.' I hesitate, wondering how much I should tell my new friend. I don't want her to think badly of me, but I would really love to talk to another dog about what happened. 'My first owners didn't really want me,' I begin, 'so I . . . sort of . . . ran away.'

Lady's round black eyes grow even wider. 'Gosh, you're brave! And you're still such a young puppy too. Whatever happened?'

I am about to launch into the story of how I found my way here, but then I feel a slight tug on my harness and I realise that Ben is leaving.

'Teddy, let's talk later,' says Lady quickly. 'I'll meet you by the fence between our gardens when I'm back from my walk, OK?'

'Come on now, Lady, stop dawdling,' mutters Tobias. I bark my goodbye. 'Great, I'll see you then!'

Ben and I make our way back up the hill towards

home, but whereas I have a new spring in my step, thanks to the excitement of finding a new friend to confide in – and such a lovely one too – his mood appears to have soured.

'That man must be the grumpiest person on the planet,' Ben mutters to himself. 'Just our luck to live next door to him.'

My happiness at meeting Lady is short-lived, however, when I get home to find Emily lying on the sofa, bundled up in a blanket. Ben obviously assumes she's asleep, as he goes straight to the kitchen to speak to Claire – 'You'll never guess what that Tobias is complaining about now!' – but when he's gone I make out a ripple of movement beneath the blanket, and then Emily's face emerges, blotchy from crying. I jump onto the sofa and straight into her outstretched arms.

'I'm scared, Teddy,' she whimpers, clutching me close. 'I don't want to go back to that hospital. I know Dr Patterson's trying to help me, but what if he tells me I have to stay in that place again?' She buries her face in my fur. 'I just don't know why I'm still feeling so ill. When you get a cold you get the sneezes and a runny nose for a few days and then you're better. Even when

I had chickenpox I was back at school in a week – and I was absolutely *covered* in spots! But it was summer when I got meningitis, and now it's Christmas, and I'm *still* not well.' She sighs. 'Everyone keeps telling me that I'll get better soon, and I just have to be patient, but what if I *never* get better? Like, ever? Then I'll never be able to ride my bicycle from Father Christmas or run around the garden with you, or go to Disneyland like Mummy and Daddy promised, because I'm going to be ill FOR EVER!'

She begins to sob again and I wonder if I should fetch Claire, but Emily is clinging on to me like I'm her only comfort, so I just snuggle in, nuzzling her, trying to show her that I'm here for her.

'I haven't said anything to Mummy or Daddy about this because I know how sad it makes them when I'm upset,' she says, sniffing. 'I'm trying to be brave and grown-up like everyone keeps telling me to be. So I think this should just be our secret, OK?'

I give her face a lick to show that I understand, and she wipes her face, cheering up at last.

'I knew you'd make me feel better; you always do. From now on I'll tell you whenever I feel scared or upset. I think that would probably help a lot. Is that all right?'

'Hey, whatever's wrong, Ems?' Claire has come in and is looking at her daughter with concern. 'Are you OK, sweetheart?'

'Teddy and I were just having a little chat,' she says.

Claire sits next to us on the sofa. 'Teddy's a good listener, aren't you, boy?' Then she puts on the smile I've noticed she uses when she's trying to jolly Emily along. 'Right, missy, we need to get going. We don't want to be late for Dr Patterson, do we?'

As Claire helps her up, Emily gives me a look that suggests she wouldn't mind in the slightest if they were late for Dr Patterson, but I'm relieved to see that at least she's got some of her fighting spirit back.

A few minutes later the family are ready to go, and while Ben puts Emily in the car Claire goes round the house and locks up. She calls me to the kitchen, obviously planning to shut me in, but remembering my promise to Lady I hover by the front door, whimpering to be let out.

'Oh, you want to stay outside, do you?' Claire considers for a moment. 'Well, I guess that fence is secure enough, and we shouldn't be too long. Be a good boy while we're gone, then – and no barking, Teddy, OK?'

I watch from the doorstep as the car pulls out of the drive. Emily waves to me from the back, and it pains me to see how anxious she looks. Perhaps I should have tried to go in the car with them, so I could keep her company? Well, it's too late now: there's nothing I can do but wait, and at least I've got my meeting with Lady to help keep my mind off what might be happening at the hospital.

I hop off onto the grass, have an invigorating nose-to-tail shake and then set off down the garden. I quickly pick up Lady's scent by the fence and call for her with a quiet woof. A few moments later I'm overjoyed to hear an answering yip, then a pair of beautiful black eyes appears in the gap between the planks.

'Hello, neighbour.' Lady smiles.

My new friend insists she wants to hear the story of how I came to be here, so I tell her all about my life with Richard and Veronica, describing the city where we lived: the enormous buildings that seemed to stretch up to the sky, the endless streets of houses and shops, the traffic and people and round-the-clock bustle.

'That sounds like it might have been London,' muses Lady. 'Tobias' daughter Anne used to live there and we would often go to visit.' She suddenly looks sad, but before I can find out why she asks, 'Do you miss it?'

'Not at all,' I say. 'I'm so much happier in the countryside – not that I ever really had the opportunity to explore the city properly.' I tell her about how Veronica used to carry me around in a handbag rather than letting me walk.

Lady laughs. 'Oh yes, that definitely sounds like London. I once saw a dog there with pink fur – can you imagine? And she actually seemed rather proud of it!'

I suppose I should be glad that at least Veronica never tried to paint me a different colour! 'Is London very far from here?' I ask.

'A very long way indeed,' says Lady, and then, without me even having to say anything, she adds softly, 'Don't worry Teddy. I very much doubt your old owners would ever be able to find you here.'

I feel a rush of gratitude towards her for putting my mind at rest. It's lovely to have another dog to talk to after such a long time without canine companionship, and Lady is obviously so wise, seeming to sense my feelings before I even share them, that I decide to talk to her about my fears over my future with the Woods.

'I can't believe how lucky I am to have ended up living with such a wonderful family,' I tell her, 'but it feels like I could be sent away at any moment. I know that Emily loves me, and I'm pretty sure that Claire and Ben like having me around too, but I'm beginning to see that they have so many problems that I'm not sure they need the added responsibility of looking after me. I'm trying very hard not to be any trouble, but I'm worried that if I put a paw wrong I'll be out.' I hesitate, trying to put my feelings into words. 'I'm sure I can help make their lives better, but I'm not exactly sure *how*.'

Lady thinks for a moment. 'From what I've seen of them they're a lovely family, but I do get the feeling that there's something missing in their lives,' she says. 'Perhaps that something is *you*, Teddy.'

I look at her quizzically. 'What do you mean?'

'For all their strengths, humans just aren't very good at living in the moment. Us dogs can take great pleasure in simply barking at a squirrel or running after a ball. We revel in the sensation of the sun warming our fur or the taste of a delicious meal—'

'Like roast chicken?' I ask eagerly.

'Yes, Teddy, like roast chicken.' Lady smiles. 'But humans spend so much of their time reflecting on the past, worrying about the future and obsessing about their problems that they tend to let the present just . . . slip away, and they don't even realise they're doing it.' She looks at me intently. 'I think you can help the Woods family by bringing their attention into the moment, so they learn to stop focusing on their worries and just enjoy life as it unfolds.'

My mind is spinning as I consider Lady's advice. Although it makes sense, I don't have any idea how to put it into practice. But then I think back to how carefree Claire and Ben seemed when we were playing together, and their obvious delight at seeing Emily's happiness as she watched me scampering after the ball. For those few moments I remember noticing that their eyes lost their usual anxious look. Perhaps all I need to do to help them is to just . . . be myself?

'You may only be young, Teddy, but I can tell you're a perceptive dog,' Lady goes on. 'I think the Woods family will quickly see how much you can bring to their lives.' She smiles again. 'So try not to worry. I really

don't think they'll send you away – in fact I'm absolutely sure of it.'

'Thank you, Lady,' I say, smiling back at my wonderful
new friend, grateful for her advice and reassurance. It's
only then that I realise I haven't asked her anything
about her life. 'I'm so sorry, I've been banging on about
myself. Please, I'd like to hear about you. Is Tobias a
kind owner?'

Lady's face clouds over.

'He is, but . . . things have changed recently.'

'What's happened?'

'A few months ago Tobias' daughter, Anne – the one
I mentioned visiting in London – died of a horrible
disease called cancer. Before she got ill, Anne used to
come and see Tobias here every few weeks. They were
very close, and he looked forward to her visits so much.
So when Anne died . . .' Lady trails off, her black eyes
full of sorrow. 'Well, Tobias took it very badly. We used
to be best friends, but since her death he's shut me
out. He doesn't talk to me any more; he doesn't talk
to anyone, really. He rarely leaves the house. I've been
with him all my life, nearly eight years now, and we've
been through so much together, but for the first time

I just don't know what to do to help him.' Her eyes glitter.

In the face of Lady's unhappiness I feel helpless. She's been so supportive to me that I would so like to do the same for her, but I have no idea what I can say to comfort her.

'I'm so sorry,' is all I eventually manage.

'Well, I'm just glad that you're here now,' says Lady, brightening up. 'It's lovely to have a friend I can talk to. Oh, I meant to ask – how are you getting on with that bad-tempered tabby cat? I've had a few run-ins with her over the years. She's not very keen on dogs, from what I can gather.'

'Martha? Yes, she can be quite tricky, but I get the impression she's a nice cat underneath it all. She's just quite elderly and prefers her own company to that of bouncy dogs.'

'Rather like Tobias then,' says Lady quietly.

Just then, as if conjured up by mention of his name, we hear Tobias calling Lady from the house.

'I'd better go,' she says. 'I've really enjoyed talking to you, Teddy.'

'Me too. I'm just sorry I couldn't help more.'

'But you did, just by listening. Let's try to talk every day, OK?'

'I'd like that very much.'

We touch noses through the gap in the fence, I get a glimpse of the white plume of her tail and then she's gone.

Left to my own devices I find plenty to do in the garden. I prowl the perimeter fence on squirrel watch (I know I can't bark, but I've been practising my growl and it's really quite menacing); I chase my tail – though frustratingly never quite manage to catch it – and I thoroughly investigate all the interesting smells I come across. One such trail leads me to a flower bed, where I pick up the faint but intriguing scent of something buried underground. With a rush of excitement, I begin to dig, hurling clods of soil onto the grass behind me. I might have thought twice about digging in the garden, but I know that Ben won't mind because he was so pleased when I helped him dig the snow off the path. *Ooh, perhaps he'll reward me with some more of that cheese, like he did last time!* The cold damp earth proves heavy going compared to snow, but digging is a very enjoyable way of burning off some of my energy, and my eventual reward is uncovering a piece of old bone, which turns out to be nicely chewable.

I'm not sure how long I'm in the garden for, but it's already getting dark by the time I hear the Woods' car turning into the drive. At once I run to greet them, desperately hoping for good news, but as soon as I see Claire's face I can tell that something is wrong. She barely manages a smile when she sees me, and there's a weariness to her movements as she gets out of the car.

I stand watching as Ben, equally sombre-faced, carries a plainly exhausted Emily into the house. I don't want to get in the way, but I'm desperate to find out what the doctor has told them.

While Ben takes Emily upstairs, I follow Claire into the kitchen, where she dumps her bag onto the table and puts the kettle on; to my dismay she seems close to tears. She doesn't seem to notice me – or is ignoring me – so I hover by the doorway, trying not to intrude.

A few moments later Ben comes into the kitchen. 'She fell asleep almost as soon as I put her in bed, poor love,' he says, sitting at the table. 'The appointment must have really taken it out of her.'

Claire leans against the counter. 'I really thought it was going to be good news,' she says, shaking her head hopelessly. 'These last few days Emily's seemed so much brighter. She's been eating better and has been far happier. I really believed we were over the worst, but now . . .'

Claire wipes her eye and Ben gets up to comfort her. 'Please try not to worry, love. Dr Patterson wants to do a few more tests, that's all. It's not necessarily bad news, he's just being careful – which is good, isn't it?'

'Yes of course, but you know how upset Emily gets about going to hospital. The idea of putting her through another round of tests and possibly more treatment after everything she's been through is heartbreaking. This has been going on for so many months now, and I can't bear the thought of her missing out on any more of her childhood.'

Ben pulls her into a hug and they stay there for a moment, Claire's head resting on his shoulder. She is clearly very upset, but although he's trying not to show it I can see how much this has affected Ben too, his jaw tense with the effort of staying strong for Claire. Oh, this is terrible. Poor Emily . . .

'I just don't understand why it's taking her so long to recover,' Claire says, her voice muffled by their embrace. 'And no one seems to have any answers! What was it that Dr Patterson said? "It's a matter of taking every day as it comes."' She gives a huff of frustration. 'It just seems so . . . so vague!'

'I know, but there's nothing we can do. We just have to stay strong to support Emily and reassure her that everything's going to be OK.' He pulls away to look into Claire's eyes, holding her shoulders. 'Because it will be, I promise.' He drops a kiss on her forehead. 'Right,' Ben goes on. 'I'm going to take the rubbish out. You make some tea, I think we could both do with a cup.'

He lifts the black bag from the bin and takes it outside, leaving Claire in the kitchen. She stares out of the window for a moment, fingering her necklace, then with a sigh starts making the tea. I'm just wondering whether now would be a good time to approach Claire and perhaps comfort her with a cuddle, when Ben shouts to her from outside. When I hear the fury in his voice, I'm instantly consumed by dread.

'Claire! Look what that bloody dog has done!'

I freeze, panic coursing through me. What in dog's name *have* I done? Surely Ben's not cross because I chewed that bit of bone . . .?

With a huff of annoyance, Claire walks to the front door and, although my instinct is to run and hide, I slink behind her, pressing myself close to the ground to show how sorry I am, even though I can't think what I've done wrong. And I've been trying so hard to be good!

When we get outside, however, it all becomes clear. Ben is gesturing angrily to the flower bed where I did my digging.

'God knows how many of the bulbs he'll have dug up,' he snaps. 'And look at the state of the lawn!'

I suppose there *is* quite a lot of soil on the grass, but I really thought that digging was allowed. Well, it doesn't matter what I thought: this has obviously made Ben very angry, and to my dismay Claire is looking irritated, too.

'Teddy, bad dog,' she says firmly. 'Look at the mess you've made!'

I hang my head in shame; I feel so terrible that I've

caused further upset to Claire and Ben after what happened at the hospital.

'As if we didn't have enough to deal with at the moment, we're having to run around after someone else's lost puppy,' says Ben, his voice getting louder and angrier. 'And I never even wanted a bloody dog in the first place!'

I turn tail and run full pelt back into the house, so scared by Ben's sudden temper that I don't even notice Martha crouching in the shadows inside the front door until she flies out of my way with a yowl. I can hear Claire shouting, but I keep running until I get to the safety of my box, where I curl up with a whimper, burying my face in my fur, trying to hide myself away. My heart is hammering and I'm shaking with fear. This has all gone so horribly wrong. I wish I could speak to Lady – I'm sure she'd know how to make things right – but for now all I can do is keep out of Claire's and Ben's way and hope they give me another chance . . .

I stay in my box for the rest of the evening – as Ben said, they have enough on their plate at the moment without having me to worry about – but I desperately miss their cuddles and kind words, and this makes me realise more than ever just how much I've come to think of myself as part of this family. If they didn't want me to live here any more, well, it just doesn't bear thinking about. I remember the conversation I had with Lady this afternoon, and how sure she had been that I could help the Woods, but right now it feels like the opposite is true: rather than making their lives better, I'm adding to their troubles.

Alone in the dark kitchen after Claire and Ben have gone to bed, I feel so lonely that I begin to whimper again. Then I become aware of a sound coming from upstairs, so quiet that at first I mistake it for branches rustling outside, but when I concentrate I realise that it's the sound of someone crying. *Emily*.

Without a second's hesitation, I jump out of my bed and race upstairs, where, by some miracle, I discover that Emily's door has been left ajar. Pushing it open with my nose, I wait in the doorway for a moment and then hear her voice in the darkness, small and trembling with tears: 'Teddy, is that you?'

I leap straight into her arms, and she pulls me close

to her, kissing my nose and rubbing her face dry on my fur. I stay happily snuggled up with her, listening to her breathing slowing and feeling her body relax into sleep, glad that I've been able to offer her some comfort. As I drift off too it occurs to me that I really shouldn't be upstairs, and that I'll be in even worse trouble than I am already if Claire or Ben finds me here, but right now my own fate seems far less important than being here for Emily. She needs me, I know that. We need each other.

❄ *Three Days Until Christmas* ❄

I'm cuddled up with my brothers and sisters next to Mum, the weight of their soft bodies supporting me. Their warmth and the rise and fall of Mum's chest have lulled me into a blissful doze. I feel so snug and content that I would be quite happy if I never had to move. But then I feel one of my littermates – probably my fidgety older brother – beginning to stir. I try to ignore him and stay exactly where I am, keeping my eyes shut and willing him back to sleep, but now the others have started to wriggle too, shifting position and jostling me, until the whole bed feels like it's alive and I have no choice but to wake up . . .

My eyes open onto darkness and it takes me a

moment to work out where I am, then Emily's scent brings me back to reality and my dream fades. She has been stirring beneath the covers but is now still, and although I long to curl up with her again among the softness of her duvet I know I should go back downstairs to the kitchen. I'm just a guest here after all; Claire and Ben have been kind enough to take me in, so it would rude of me not to stick to their rules, especially after yesterday's digging disgrace.

There is no sign of Martha as I make my way down-stairs – she must be outside hunting – and I find myself almost longing for a glimpse of her yellowy-green eyes in the shadows, as at least then I wouldn't feel quite so alone. Down in the kitchen though all is still, so I settle in my box by the Aga, close my eyes and quickly fall back asleep.

To my relief, Claire doesn't seem quite so upset – nor quite so cross with me – when she comes down to the kitchen this morning. She picks me up for a cuddle and says an approving 'Good boy, Teddy' when I sit patiently while she's preparing my breakfast. It takes every scrap of my willpower not to jump up, because she's making my favourite – scrambled eggs – and the smell alone is making me want to gallop around the kitchen in anticipation, but I've decided I must be extra-careful today to avoid getting into mischief. In the light of what happened yesterday, I want to show Claire and Ben that I'm no trouble, but am in fact a pleasure to have around.

When Claire lets me out into the garden I notice that the heap of earth I threw onto the grass yesterday has disappeared; Ben must have cleared it up last night. I feel another pang of guilt. If only I could explain that I wasn't trying to be naughty! Perhaps if they knew how hard I'm trying to behave, they might be more understanding when I do mess up.

Emily doesn't appear for breakfast, but I notice Ben taking her up a bowl of cereal and returning a little later with it largely untouched.

'She says she's not hungry,' he tells Claire. He looks worried.

'Don't worry, I'll take her up some fruit in a bit,' she says, touching his hand and smiling to reassure him, but I can tell she's concerned too.

This is not good. Emily must be feeling ill again. Even the fact that I get to eat her leftover milk-soaked cereal does little to cheer me up. I'm worried about her, especially after the trauma of yesterday, so when Claire and Ben are busy downstairs, I creep up to see how she's getting on. She's lying in bed, but to my delight she's awake.

'Teddy!' She breaks into a smile, holding out a hand to me. I stay on the floor by the bed, snuffling her fingers and letting her stroke me; I don't want to jump up if she's feeling out of sorts.

'Thank you for coming up to see me last night,' she says in a hushed voice. 'I didn't tell Mummy about it because I thought she might be cross with you after what happened with Daddy's flower bed.' Emily opens her eyes wide. 'Never dig in Daddy's flower beds, Teddy,' she whispers solemnly. 'He is *very* particular about his garden. And don't pick any of his flowers either – that makes him cross too, even if you're doing it as a nice surprise for Mummy . . .'

I wag my tail, hoping she can tell that I'm sorry for what happened.

'It's OK, Teddy. I know you're a good boy.' She rests

her head back on the pillow; she looks very pale this morning.

'Ah, so you've got a visitor have you?' I turn to see Claire standing in the bedroom doorway. Thankfully she doesn't seem to mind that I'm up here. 'I've brought you some apple and banana, Ems. Do you think you could manage a bit?'

Emily shrugs. 'I'll try.'

'Attagirl. We need to keep your strength up, as we're going to do the Christmas food shop in a little while, and I know you won't want to miss that, will you?'

Emily's face brightens. 'Are we going to get the turkey?'

'Yes, it's waiting for us at the butcher's.'

'And the Christmas cake?'

'No, I've made that myself this year,' says Claire proudly. 'It's sitting downstairs in the kitchen, ready to be iced. You can help me this afternoon if you like, love?'

'Yes please,' says Emily. 'I'm very good at cooking, aren't I, Mummy? Especially the licking-the-bowl bit.'

'You certainly are. Right, I'd better take Teddy out for a walk, because he's going to have to stay here while we go shopping, and we need to get rid of some of that excess energy, don't we, boy?'

Emily looks at me and then at her mum. 'Is Daddy still cross with Teddy?'

Claire smiles. 'No, I'm sure he's forgiven him now. He knows that Teddy didn't mean to be naughty.'

Really? This is fantastic news! Ben seemed so angry yesterday I felt sure it would take a few days for him to forgive me.

'I think we'll keep Teddy inside while we're out this morning, though,' Claire goes on, tickling me under my chin. 'Just to make sure we don't have any more little . . . incidents.'

Back downstairs, Claire puts on her biggest coat and warmest boots – it must be cold out, because I noticed a few flakes of snow drifting past the window earlier – and then she fixes my red-ribbon harness on and we set off down the lane. As we pass Tobias' house I'm delighted to spot Lady sitting in the front window, and I bark 'Good morning' at her. With any luck we'll be able to speak by the fence this afternoon.

I might be imagining it, but I'm feeling much steadier on my paws today, as if suddenly I've done a lot of growing-up, and I feel very proud to be walking along by Claire's side as if we're officially dog and owner – even more so when we pass a few of the Woods' other neighbours, and they all say admiring things about me. One lady even asks if she can take me home with her, and when Claire answers, 'Unfortunately not, because Teddy's becoming one of the family, aren't you, boy?' I can't help but give an answering bark of happiness. Just a few hours ago I thought Claire and Ben might send me to the council kennels, but now I have a vision of myself as a grown-up dog curled at Emily's feet by the fire, and, as we head back up the hill towards Glebe Cottage, I remember Lady's words yesterday afternoon: 'I think the Woods family will quickly see how much you can bring to their lives.' At the time I wasn't convinced, but now I'm beginning to believe it might be possible.

By the time we get home Ben has got Emily up and dressed, and she is waiting on the sofa. She still looks very pale and a little wobbly, but Ben has told her she can choose the 'Christmas crackers' (whatever they are) when they get to the shops, and her excitement about that is obviously helping take her mind off how she's feeling.

'Right, Teddy, you behave yourself while we're out, please,' says Ben as Claire helps Emily to the door, and I wag my tail to show him that I fully intend to be an excellent guard dog and look after the house to the very best of my abilities.

'I'll bring you a Christmas bone from the butcher's,' calls Emily, waving to me as she leaves.

'Martha, you're in charge,' says Ben with a smile, and I look round to see the tabby cat sitting on the stairs, surveying the room in her usual enigmatic manner.

As ever, Martha's arrival makes me feel both pleased and concerned: on the one hand it means we have another chance for a fresh start – because I feel sure, given time, that we can be friends – on the other, I still remember how much my nose hurt after our first encounter.

'Play nicely, you two,' says Ben. 'We'll see you in a couple of hours.'

And with that the door closes behind him, and Martha and I are left alone.

I look over to her, my head to one side and tail wagging in a friendly fashion. It would be nice if we could hang out together, but she's ignoring me so I decide to go back to bed for a nap. After all, there's no way I can get into trouble if I'm asleep.

As soon as I've got comfortable in my box, however, Martha appears in the kitchen doorway. She stops and takes a long, hard look in my direction, her tail swishing from side to side, then walks towards me, sits on the floor and turns her attention to washing herself. Well, this *is* a nice surprise – it's almost as if she'd like some company too! Perhaps, if she's feeling better disposed towards me today, now might be a good time to try to make friends?

Moving very slowly so as not to startle her, I climb out of my box, one paw at a time, and stand on the floor, looking at her expectantly. She carries on with her washing, but her eyes have now flicked towards me; she's not exactly giving off friendly vibes, but I think that's just her way, and I have to remember that cats are naturally quite aloof. I shouldn't judge her by the same criteria as I would another dog, as we do tend to be more sociable creatures.

Encouraged (well, not actively discouraged, at least), I take a tentative step towards her. She freezes mid-wash, still staring at me, but stays where she is. Yes, this is promising; she definitely seems more comfortable being around me. Won't Claire and Ben be pleased if they come home to find Martha and I snuggled up together like best friends? I wag my tail happily at the thought and take another step towards her – then suddenly, as if spooked, Martha takes a flying leap up onto the counter, as quick as a squirrel up a tree, barely missing a box that's sitting near the edge of the worktop. She stares at me, her eyes wide with annoyance, and, cowed by her glare, I sit back down with a whimper, feeling like I've just been thoroughly told off.

What happens next is such a blur that I'm not entirely sure whether or not it's an accident, but one moment Martha lifts her paw as if to resume her washing and then the next the box that was sitting close to her on the counter comes tumbling down to the floor. To make matters worse, the box was obviously not closed properly, and as it falls a great cloud of white, sweet-smelling powder spills out, covering the kitchen floor like a snowdrift. It would look quite pretty if it hadn't made such an awful mess.

For a moment I just sit there, stunned, while Martha crouches on the counter looking down at the white blanket, her tail flicking from side to side. Surely she didn't mean to deliberately knock the box off? I find it impossible to tell from her expression, which seems more interested than remorseful, but either way this does not look at all good. I'm not to blame for this mess, but Claire and Ben aren't going to know that, are they?

There's so much of the stuff on the floor that I decide my only option is to try clearing it up; after all, it worked with the snow on the garden path. So I scrabble at the powder with my front paws, but instead of landing in a neat heap like the snow, all I succeed in doing is sending clouds of it up into the air, sprinkling it over even more of the room and making my nose itch horribly. *Aaaa-choo!* I sneeze three times and fall over in a heap. Great, now it's all over my fur as well as the floor!

Perhaps I should try licking it up? Cautiously, I run my tongue over the floor. This stuff, whatever it is, is extremely tasty, but I'm too anxious to enjoy it, as all I can think about is how angry Ben and Claire are going to be when they get home and see the state of the kitchen. To make matters worse, I soon discover that licking the powder makes it go all gooey and sticky, which is making even more of a mess; besides, there's far too much of it to eat by myself. I look round at Martha, wondering if she might help, but she's staring through the window at a bird in the garden. She seems completely unconcerned about what's happened, which actually reassures me a little. Perhaps I'm worrying unnecessarily, and the Woods won't mind about this too much? They might even see the funny side! Yes, maybe the sensible thing to do is just stick to my original plan and have a nap until they return.

But as I settle back in my bed, I see Martha delicately picking her way along the counter towards something I hadn't noticed before now: a large brown cake sitting on the side near the Aga. Judging by its treacly, spicy scent and the way it's presented on a fancy stand as if it's extremely important, I'm guessing this must be the Christmas cake that Claire was talking about earlier. No wonder Emily is looking forward to Christmas so much – it smells amazing! Martha obviously thinks so too, as she is now standing right next to the stand and craning her head up, sniffing at the cake, and then, as I watch, she opens her mouth and, to my utter amazement, stretches out her little pink tongue towards it.

Well, I may only be young, but after the incident with the candy canes on the tree I know all too well that you shouldn't help yourself to food without it being offered, even if it is sitting there looking like it wants to be eaten, so I let out a volley of barks to warn Martha to stop, but she doesn't even flinch. The one time I'd actually quite like to scare her and she completely ignores me!

Luckily, thanks to the height of the stand, she can't quite reach the cake, and I'm just breathing out a sigh of relief when to my horror Martha rears back on her haunches, places her front paws up onto the stand and leans towards the cake. Suddenly the stand topples towards her, the cake slides off and then smashes on the floor, shattering into pieces. With a yowl of fright, Martha skitters along the counter and takes a flying leap out of the door and into the living room, and a few moments later I hear the soft *thunk* of the cat flap.

My heart pounding, I look around at the state of the kitchen: the white powder spilled over the floor dotted with my paw prints, the sticky licked-up patches and now the scattered rubble of the cake. Somehow, I think it's unlikely that Ben and Claire will be able to see the funny side of this because, well, there really is no funny side. This is a disaster. The kitchen is a mess, the Christmas cake has been destroyed and, in the absence of Martha, there's only one explanation for this whole shambles: me.

The thought of how they will react when they come home is terrifying; perhaps I'd be better off running away right now? But I can't fit through the cat flap (I've tried already and nearly got stuck), and besides I love it here. I don't want to leave. So all I can do is sit and wait and hope that Claire and Ben somehow know this wasn't my fault.

Without a clue how I can make things better, I climb back into my box. I must have fallen asleep because a little while later I open my eyes and for a moment I'm shocked all over again at the sight of the kitchen. Then I remember what happened and sink my head back on my paws with a whimper. They're going to send me away this time, aren't they? They won't have any choice.

Then as I lie there, miserably pondering my fate and planning my escape route (because I *really* don't like the sound of those council kennels), I realise that I'm not alone in the kitchen after all. A small brown mouse has emerged from under the counter and is now making its way through the white powder towards the cake, seemingly unworried that it's scurrying about right under my nose. Well, that's just too much for me: with a woof of fury I leap out of my bed and give chase. The cake might be ruined, but the least I can do is protect the crumbs!

The mouse abruptly turns and runs out of the kitchen, surprisingly speedily for something so tiny, into the living room, where it disappears into the pile of presents underneath the Christmas tree. Driven on by my instincts, I plough in after it, sending the presents flying as I scrabble around trying to follow its trail. Too late, I realise that the space under the tree isn't quite big enough for a small-ish puppy. Too late I remember that I'm supposed to be on my very best behaviour, and too late I notice the tree begin to topple . . .

When everything falls still and silent again, I force myself to open my eyes. *Oh no.* No no no. The Christmas tree lies on the floor, decorations scattered around it; its lights flicker for a moment and then go off. The presents, some of which look worryingly bashed-up, have been flung around the room, and there is a trail of white puppy-shaped paw prints leading from the kitchen to where I'm standing amid the chaos. The mouse, however, is nowhere to be seen.

Just at that moment I hear the sound of a car pulling into the drive. Seconds later there's the crunch of feet on the gravel and then, before I can think what to do, there's the click of the key in the lock and the front door swings open.

'Hello, Teddy, we're h——'

Claire's mouth falls open and the bags she's holding drop to the floor, their contents spilling out onto the doorstep, but she doesn't seem to notice. She just stands there, staring at the fallen tree, her eyes popping.

I try to explain what has happened. 'A mouse!' I bark to her. 'It was a mouse, trying to eat the Christmas cake!'

But of course she doesn't understand; besides, I probably shouldn't mention the Christmas cake, as that's hardly good news either . . .

Claire's still frozen, speechless, in the doorway, when Ben and Emily appear behind her.

'Oh my God,' exclaims Ben, his face furious. 'What the hell has that blasted dog done now!'

'Daddy, don't say bad words,' scolds Emily.

'He's killed the bloody Christmas tree!' he shouts.

I cower by the sofa, racked with guilt, trying to make myself as small as possible. Claire still hasn't said anything, which I suppose might possibly be a good sign, but she's looking horrified. The only small comfort is that Emily doesn't seem too upset about the tree.

'And what's that all over the floor?' says Ben, storming into the kitchen on the trail of my footprints. I hear him gasp and then mutter, 'That bloody dog . . .'

Claire follows him through the mess of fallen Christmas decorations to the kitchen, and when she sees the white powder and broken cake she finally breaks her silence.

'Teddy,' she says quietly, turning back to look at me. 'What have you *done*?'

She doesn't sound angry, but the disappointment and unhappiness in her voice make me feel ten times worse than if she had shouted. I'm supposed to be helping this family, but instead I just seem to be upsetting them!

'What's that white stuff?' asks Emily.

'Icing sugar,' says Ben.

'My cake,' murmurs Claire. 'The first Christmas cake I ever made!'

'It's OK, love,' says Ben, putting his arm around her. 'We've got lots of mince pies, and there's always the Christmas pudding—'

'I HATE Christmas pudding,' says Emily.

'Ems, now is not the time,' says Ben, a warning note in his voice.

'But how did Teddy knock over the cake? It was on the side,' mutters Claire. 'And the icing sugar?'

'He must have jumped up,' says Ben.

Claire shakes her head. 'No, he's never jumped on the side before.'

'Not when *we've* been here,' says Ben. 'God only knows what he gets up to when we're not around.'

'Maybe Teddy didn't do it,' says Emily. 'Perhaps it was Martha.'

At the mention of Martha's name, I can't stop myself from giving a little woof. Surely I shouldn't have to take *all* the blame for this? I don't want to get her into trouble, even though I'm still not sure whether she deliberately knocked off the box of icing sugar, but I know the Woods would never send Martha away, whatever trouble she got into. She's far more part of the family than I am.

'I hardly think the cat would have caused all of this mess,' says Ben, ignoring my bark. 'Martha's never done anything like this before, and she doesn't even like cake.'

If only you knew, I think to myself.

'Besides, those are clearly dog paw prints all over the floor, not cat,' Ben goes on. Martha cleverly managed to flee the kitchen without setting a paw in the sugar. He shakes his head angrily. 'I'm going to call the council and ask if they can take Teddy tomorrow. We've got enough on our plate without . . .' He waves his arms at the mess. 'Without all *this*.'

Emily looks horrified. 'Daddy, no, you can't send Teddy away!'

'Sweetheart, I'm sorry, but he was never ours to keep,' says Ben. 'We tried to make it work, but our priority has to be looking after you, not clearing up after Teddy.'

'Please, Daddy, don't make him leave! Teddy's my best friend!' Emily clings on to her dad's arm. 'I've felt so much better since he got here, you can't send him to the kennels.'

'I promise we'll talk about getting another pet once you're feeling better,' says Ben.

'But you don't understand! I won't ever get better if Teddy's not here!'

Ben sighs. 'Come on now, Emily, don't be silly—'

'I'm NOT being silly; it's true!' And she begins to cry, her whole body shaking with desperate sobs. 'Don't you *want* me to get better?'

I sink to the floor with a whimper. This is all my fault. I glance over to the front door, which has been left open. I could easily slip away now and spare this family any more trouble. Perhaps I'd be lucky and find another wonderful home . . . And then I look back to where Ben and Claire are trying to comfort the wailing Emily, and my heart lurches horribly. I don't want another home; I want to stay here. I have such a strong sense that this is meant to be where I belong, but how can I make things right again?

Claire has now picked up Emily, who is sobbing into her mum's shoulder. 'Sweetheart, shhh, it's OK,' she says. 'Of course Daddy and I want you to get better, more than anything – and you *will* get better, I promise – but while you're still poorly, we need to be able to focus on looking after you. I know how much you love Teddy, we all do, but puppies need a lot of care, and it's not fair on him if we can't give him the attention and exercise he needs. Wouldn't it be better if we found him a lovely home with a family who have the time look after him properly?

'No,' says Emily, her voice muffled by Claire's jumper. 'Teddy doesn't want another home; he wants to stay here, with me.'

Claire looks at Ben, who shrugs helplessly.

'I tell you what, sweetheart: why don't we go upstairs and I'll put a Disney DVD on for you,' says Claire. 'It's been a busy morning, and you could probably do with a rest. Daddy and I will sort out the Christmas tree, then we can all talk about Teddy later, OK?'

Emily raises her head from her mum's shoulder. 'Promise you won't send him away?'

Claire and Ben exchange glances again.

'We'll see,' says Claire eventually. 'Everything will be all right though, I promise you.'

Emily yawns; she looks too tired to put up a fight. 'OK,' she mumbles, rubbing her eyes.

While Claire takes Emily upstairs to her bedroom,

Ben comes to find me in the living room, grumbling something about 'the last thing we need' as he picks his way through the jumble of presents, lights and decorations.

'Right, you. Outside while we decide what we're going to do with you,' he says, shooing me out into the front garden. 'See if you can manage to stay out of trouble while Claire and I clear up this mess.'

As the door closes behind me I get a final glimpse of Ben's face, his expression grim, and I can't help wondering whether I've seen the last of his smiles. He's forgiven me before, but I have a horrible feeling that this will be one disgrace too many. With only a few days until Christmas, I've presided over the destruction of the Christmas tree *and* Claire's cake. Some guard dog I turned out to be!

I'm too worried to take my usual exploratory tour of the garden and have no energy for scampering or tail-chasing, so I lie down on the doorstep, half-hoping that Claire will have a change of heart and come out to get me – because surely she must know, deep down, that I'm not a bad dog – but the door remains firmly closed. Although I can hear movement and the murmur of conversation from inside I feel as alone and as hopeless as I did on that dark snowy night when I first arrived at the Woods' door. I curl up in a furry ball, trying to keep warm, and prepare myself for a long wait.

Then suddenly I hear the most wonderful noise – a soft yip on the other side of the fence – and my head flies up and my heart gives a little leap of joy. *Lady!* Oh thank goodness. If anyone can help me feel better, it's her. I scamper down the garden as fast as I can, and there she is, waiting for me on the other side of the fence, her black eyes bright and full of affection.

'Lady! I'm so glad to see you.' We greet each other by touching noses through the gap in the fence; her scent instantly calms and comforts me. 'I'm afraid I've made the most terrible mess of things,' I tell her, sitting down.

'What's happened, Teddy?'

'I've ruined the Woods' Christmas,' I say miserably. 'I've ruined *everything*.'

With her gentle encouragement, I tell Lady about what happened with Martha and the mouse – 'I *told* you that cat was trouble,' she says, shaking her head – and what Ben said about sending me to the kennels.

'If it wasn't for Emily sticking up for me, I think their minds would already be made up,' I say. 'Whatever can I do to make it better? I'm scared, Lady. I feel so sure that I'm meant to be their dog, but I really think they're going to send me away this time.'

'Oh Teddy, I'm so sorry,' she says, nuzzling me through the fence. 'It's unfair that you're getting the blame, but you do need to work on controlling your instincts too. You're still very young, and it does take a while for a dog to learn to live alongside humans and follow all their confusing rules. I remember getting into all sorts of scrapes when I first came to live with Tobias.'

'Really?' I find that quite a surprise, judging by how poised Lady is now. 'But how did you learn what was right and what was wrong?'

'Oh, trial and error, mostly.'

'I don't think I'm going to get that opportunity,' I say miserably. 'I'm pretty sure I've already had my trial and made too many errors.'

Lady just looks at me for a moment, as if in thought. 'I've got an idea,' she says eventually. 'How about I teach you a little of what I know about living with humans? Just the basics, obviously, and I'm no expert, but it might just help. Only if you'd like me to . . .'

'Yes please!' I feel a surge of gratitude. 'If you're sure you don't mind, that would be amazing. Thank you so much!'

Lady smiles. 'Wonderful. OK, well, let's start with the basics. Is there anything you're particularly confused by?'

'The "Sit" thing,' I reply at once. 'Why do humans keep telling us to "Sit"?'

'Ah, yes, the great "Sit" mystery.' Lady smiles. 'Of all the things we have to learn about humans, that must be one of the most confusing. If it's any comfort, Teddy, every dog, whatever her breed or background, finds it equally strange.'

'But what does it *mean*? It seems so important to humans, I know they must want us to do something other than just sit down.'

'But that's exactly what it means,' says Lady.

'What, literally just sit? Even if standing is more convenient?'

'Yes.'

I hesitate for a moment, trying to get my head around

this bizarre concept. 'But . . . why? I completely understand why we have to come when we're called, but the
sitting thing just seems so . . . pointless.'

Lady smiles at my confusion. 'What you must
remember is that while humans love us, they also like
to know that they're in charge – well, *think* they're in
charge, at least. Telling us to sit is their way of checking
that we're paying attention to them. And it makes them
so happy when we do it that it's worth playing along,
just like when they tell us to "Fetch."'

'Ah, now that one I *do* understand,' I say excitedly.
'It's a game, isn't it? They throw something, then we
bring it back to them again, and so on.'

'Absolutely. Well done, Teddy,' says Lady, and I glow
with pride at her praise. 'And there are other more
advanced yet seemingly pointless commands too,' she
goes on, 'such as "Roll over" and "Heel," but I think
that's for another time. What else would you like to
know about?'

'Digging,' I say and explain about Ben's wildly different reactions to my two attempts in the garden. 'Is
it acceptable behaviour or not?'

'My advice would be never to dig unless you're

explicitly told otherwise,' says Lady. 'Humans generally disapprove of behaviour that makes a mess or destroys things, which means digging is usually deemed unacceptable – as is, of course, chewing.'

'Mmmm, I learned about that the hard way,' I say, wincing at the memory of Veronica's shoe. 'But some things are OK to chew, right?'

'Yes, generally bones, sticks and toys, but – and this is very important – only toys that are given to you with the express purpose of being chewed. You mustn't chew any of Emily's toys, for instance.'

I nod, taking in Lady's advice.

'Now, are you clear on what I call "no-go zones"?' asks Lady.

'What are those?'

'Places where humans can sit but dogs aren't allowed: beds, sofas, that sort of thing. This can get particularly confusing because in some circumstances a no-go zone will suddenly become a go-zone, for reasons that are only clear to the humans themselves, before becoming a no-go zone again.'

I'm afraid this makes no sense to me at all, and I apologetically tell Lady as much.

'OK, well, your owner might tell you off for jumping up on the sofa, but then one evening they'll be sitting on the very same sofa watching television and encourage you to sit on their lap. Should you jump up or not?'

My head is spinning. 'Um . . . no?'

Lady smiles. 'Wrong, I'm afraid. If your human invites you onto a sofa or bed you are allowed on there, but you must always wait to be asked.'

I think back to my late-night visit to Emily's bed and am relieved that I managed to get back downstairs without Claire or Ben finding out.

'Thank you so much, Lady. This will definitely help me stay out of trouble if the Woods decide to keep me . . .' I tail off, the doubt over my future hitting me like a brick all over again. '*Do* you think the Woods will keep me?'

To my concern, Lady now seems a little lost for words. 'I really don't know,' she says eventually. 'They sound like they have so many worries at the moment, and I know humans can get quite overwhelmed, but hopefully they'll realise you're still a puppy and didn't mean to cause any harm.'

'Is there anything I can do to make things right?'

Lady puts her head on one side as if considering my question. 'What do you think would make the Woods' lives better?'

'For me not to mess the house up?'

She smiles. 'Apart from that.'

I think for a moment. 'Ben and Claire need to know that Emily will be OK. They're worried about money too, but Emily is their biggest worry. I think that's why they always seem so stressed. If Emily was well again I'm sure they'd be able to cope with everything else.' I hesitate. 'Including me, perhaps.'

'So be there for Emily. Do everything you can to help her get stronger.'

'I will,' I say firmly.

'And trust that Claire and Ben will realise how much you can bring to their lives.'

'OK,' I say. 'I'll try my best.'

'Oh, and Teddy? Remember to sit when they tell you to,' Lady finishes with a smile.

It's dark by the time Claire finally calls me back inside the house. I creep gingerly into the living room, keeping my head lowered and my tail wagging a sincere apology, to be greeted by the marvellous sight of the Christmas tree standing in the corner, its decorations and lights back in place and the presents sitting in a neat pile at its foot.

I glance up at Claire, who raises her eyebrows at me. 'Good as new, eh Teddy?'

But while I long for her to scoop me up in her arms, to nuzzle my fur and tell me everything will be OK, she doesn't even give me a stroke. Meanwhile, Ben is sitting on the sofa reading the newspaper and barely looks up when I come in; clearly I haven't been forgiven. Then I notice that Ben isn't alone on the sofa: Martha is curled up on his lap, her purr rumbling in her chest like a miniature tractor as he scratches behind her ear. When she hears me she opens her eyes, briefly, and then closes them again, a look of contentment on her face.

I wonder if Martha has any idea how much trouble I'm in? I feel a flash of annoyance. Most of this mess was *her* fault, after all, yet I'm getting all the blame!

The kitchen floor is spotless, as if nothing untoward has gone on in there, but the empty cake stand still sits accusingly on the side. I can smell that Martha's food bowl has recently been filled (and emptied), but there's obviously going to be no dinner for me tonight. That's OK – I don't have much of an appetite anyway. I can still taste the sickly sweetness of that icing sugar, reminding me of the day's traumas.

That evening nothing is said about what will happen to me. Claire and Ben all but ignore me as they have their supper and tidy up the kitchen, and I make sure I stay out of their way as much as possible. I keep hoping I might have the opportunity to show off my new obedience skills, but sadly neither Claire nor Ben have cause to tell me to 'Sit.' It looks like I will have to wait until tomorrow morning to find out whether or not I'll be able to stay. I try to keep Lady's advice in mind and trust that they'll forgive me, but as they turn off the lights and lock up I'm hit by such a wave of sadness that it feels like my heart is going to break. I wonder how on earth I'll get through the night on my own, so as soon as the house falls silent I get out of bed and creep straight upstairs to Emily. No-go zone or not, I need a hug.

'I knew you'd come to see me, Teddy,' she whispers, clearly as pleased to see me as I am her. 'I told Mummy I wanted to keep my door open in case I had a nightmare, but really it was so you could get in.'

I burrow under the duvet and curl up against the curve of her tummy. At moments like this, when everything seems so perfectly right with the world, it's easy to forget how precarious my situation is.

Emily sighs. 'I don't know what I'd do if I didn't have you, Teddy.'

I nuzzle my nose against her tummy to try to reassure her. Even if I don't entirely believe it myself, I want her to believe that everything will be OK. The most important thing is Emily's happiness.

'You're *meant* to be my dog; I know it,' she says, wrapping her arms around me. 'Father Christmas brought you here to help make me better – that's why you were on our doorstep. I told that to Mummy and Daddy this afternoon.' She yawns, snuggling closer to me. 'I said to them, "Teddy has to stay with us because Father Christmas wants him to."'

The sound of her voice soothes me, and I can feel myself drifting off to sleep.

'Grown-ups can sometimes get a bit confused, Teddy,' says Emily, her voice now coming to me as if from very far away. 'But I think Mummy and Daddy will come to see that I'm absolutely right . . .'

❄ *Two Days Until Christmas* ❄

When I wake I'm still in the same position, curled up against Emily's belly, but rather than being gorgeously warm and snuggly like I was at bedtime, I am now way too hot – suffocating, in fact. *I've got to get out of here!* Feeling panicked, I fight my way out from underneath Emily's duvet and wriggle on top of the covers, immediately relieved by the coolness of the air in her bedroom. *Phew, that's better!* I glance at the window. It's still dark, but there's a greyish-white light creeping around the edge of the curtains which suggests morning isn't far away, so I reluctantly decide that I should go back downstairs, as I don't want Claire and Ben to find me up here when they wake up. Emily is stirring, and so, in the hope of a goodbye kiss, I make my way up the bed to her pillow – with some difficulty, as the duvet is so squishy it reminds me of trying to walk through snow – but even before I reach her, I realise something is terribly wrong.

She is trembling and mumbling to herself as if she's having a nightmare, but to my surprise her eyes are wide open, and as I get closer to her I can feel the heat radiating from her forehead. No wonder I was so uncomfortable in bed: Emily's skin feels hotter than the Aga! That's not normal, I'm sure of it.

I nuzzle at her to check if she's OK and when she doesn't acknowledge me I give a little woof, but she still doesn't answer. In fact, even though her eyes are open she doesn't seem to notice me at all. She's tossing from side to side, and even in the dim early-morning light I can see that her face is pale and sweaty. I bark again, louder this time, but she still doesn't respond.

Without a second thought, I jump off Emily's bed and race down the corridor towards Ben and Claire's room to get help. Martha has obviously been in her favourite spot on the landing, because as I run past she flies out of the way with a yowl of indignation.

The last I see of her is her white-tipped tail bobbing downstairs.

Ben and Claire's bedroom door is shut, so I scrabble against it and bark at full volume, desperately trying to raise the alarm. After a little while I hear movement inside in the room and Ben's voice – 'Not again! That bloody dog' – and then the door opens and he emerges, his hair standing on end. He looks livid, but I can't worry about that now. All that matters is making him understand that Emily is ill.

I give another volley of barks, hoping that Ben will be able to detect the alarm in my voice, but instead he scoops me up and, to my horror, heads grumpily downstairs. I wriggle and kick my legs, desperately trying to communicate that this is an emergency, but he just grips me even more tightly, muttering angrily to himself about kennels.

'You stay in there, and I'll deal with you in the morning,' he says, almost throwing me into the kitchen, and then slams the door shut behind him.

Oh no! I scratch at the door, barking furiously, but Ben just shouts at me as he heads back upstairs – 'For God's sake, be QUIET!' – and then the sound of his footsteps fades into silence and I'm left frantically pacing around the kitchen in a frenzy of panic. What on earth am I going to do now?

My insides feel so jittery that I'm struggling to focus. Come on, Teddy, you need to calm down, because going to pieces isn't going to help Emily, is it? I make myself sit down by the door and consider my options, trying to imagine what Lady might do in this situation.

I could keep trying to raise the alarm, but I get the impression that my barking would be emphatically ignored, so I think that should probably be a last resort. My second option is escape: if I could get out of the kitchen and go back upstairs maybe I can lead Ben and Claire to Emily's room. But one glance at the heavy wooden door tells me that this is impossible. Even if I could jump high enough to reach the latch – which I can't – I don't have a clue how to open it. No, I definitely won't be able to get out of here on my own. I suppose I could just wait here until the morning, which is surely only an hour or so away now, and hope that Emily will be OK until her parents go in to wake her up. Maybe I've been worrying unnecessarily, and there's nothing seriously wrong with her? Then I think back to her blank stare and her hot clammy skin, and a bolt of fear shoots through me. There's no doubt that she needs help right now.

Then, just as I decide that I'll have to start barking again, because I can't just sit here doing nothing while Emily gets worse, I notice a flicker of movement in the shadows, and look round to discover Martha crouched on top of the counter. *Thank goodness!* She's looking at me with her usual expression of disdain tinged with fear, but right now I don't care what she does to me: with her help, I might just have a chance of getting out of here so that I can raise the alarm!

The challenge is to communicate all of this to Martha as quickly as possible, and I find myself wishing I'd paid more attention when my mother taught us about cats. I remember the bit about steering well clear if they were arching their backs and hissing, but asking them for help in an emergency? Not so much. Then it occurs to me that just as I can often sense another animal's or human's emotions, perhaps cats have that gift too? Maybe, if I demonstrate to Martha how desperate I am to get out of the kitchen, she might realise that there's a reason for my panic and help me out. I know she doesn't want to be friends with me, but I'm sure that deep down she loves Emily just as much as I do; she's known her since she was a baby, after all.

Standing by the door, I woof at Martha, wagging my tail. She recoils, still staring at me, so I give another sharp bark and then scratch at the door, hoping she'll understand, although I actually have no idea whether she knows how to open the door either. Martha doesn't move, but at least she's now watching me with interest. That's a start at least! I keep scrabbling at the door and whimpering, trying my hardest to get across the urgency of the situation.

'We need to open the door,' I bark, knowing she won't understand me but desperate to get the message through. 'Emily needs our help. She's very ill! Please, Martha . . .'

Then a miracle happens. In an instant Martha's manner is dramatically transformed: her usual haughty expression vanishes and that nervy skittishness that always makes me worry what she might do next is replaced with an air of calm determination. Without a moment's hesitation, she gets up from where she's crouching and pads around the kitchen counter until she's standing directly above me, right next to the door. If I didn't know better, I would assume she's understood everything I just said to her. It occurs to me that perhaps she did understand me after all: just because I can't speak cat, it doesn't mean that Martha – who is, after all, considerably older and more experienced than I am – doesn't understand dog.

With a rush of excitement, I woof at her again.

'Can you open it?' I ask. 'Do you know how to work the latch?'

And this time, to my astonishment, I feel sure that Martha has understood. She inclines her head ever so slightly towards me, almost as if she's nodding in the same way a human might, and then rears back on her haunches on the countertop and stretches up until she can reach the latch with her front paws, pressing down on it with as much force as she can muster. I watch, barely daring to breathe, as the latch shifts ever so slightly, but before Martha manages to open it her paws slip and she nearly tumbles off the counter. I yelp, but of course I didn't count on her superior balancing skills and she manages not to fall. Looking slightly embarrassed, she sits down on the counter and begins to wash herself.

'Come on, you can do it. Try again!' I bark eagerly.

At this Martha stops washing and gives me a cold stare.

'Sorry. Please try again,' I add quickly, remembering my manners.

So she does, and this time, incredibly, she manages to push down the latch enough for it to click free, and the door swings open.

Pausing just long enough to bark my gratitude to Martha, I race through the living room and then tackle the stairs as quickly as I can – which actually is frustratingly slowly because I still haven't got the hang of moving my paws the right way, but at least I only lose my footing a couple of times. When I get to the top Martha is already sitting up there waiting for me. How on earth does she do that? I'm beginning to think that she has special cat powers that I can't begin to understand.

Under her concerned eye, I run across the landing to Ben and Claire's door and start barking and scrabbling, even more urgently than before, and this time it only takes a matter of seconds before there's the sound of stirring and Claire's muffled 'But how did he get out?' followed by Ben grumbling, 'I could have sworn I made sure the door was shut,' and then I hear feet stamping across the floor. The door is flung open and Ben appears, eyes popping with rage, Claire peering over his shoulder, looking just as sleep-rumpled and thunderous.

'So help me, Teddy, if you don't—' begins Ben angrily, reaching down to grab me.

This time, however, I'm ready for him. I dodge his hands and bound off towards Emily's room, willing them to follow me.

'Teddy, come here NOW!' calls Claire sharply.

But I don't stop until I reach the foot of Emily's bed, where I sit and begin to howl. Moments later Ben and Claire race into the room, their faces furious.

'Right,' splutters Ben. 'You're going outside, and then as soon as the council kennels open I'm—'

'Ben, wait,' says Claire, her voice tinged with worry. 'Look, something's wrong with Emily.'

My bad behaviour instantly forgotten, they swiftly cross to the bed, where Emily is still twisting and mumbling, her eyes fixed in that same blank stare. Claire puts her hand on her daughter's forehead.

'Oh my God, she's burning up,' she gasps. 'Emily? Darling, can you hear me?' She grabs her shoulders and gives her a slight shake, looking increasingly concerned. 'Wake up, Ems, please! Darling? Emily?' When there's still no response, she turns to Ben, her face etched with fear.

'We've got to get her to hospital,' she says.

At first it doesn't seem as if Ben has heard her; he stays rooted to the spot, staring at his daughter.

'Ben?' Claire's voice is urgent and edged with panic. 'We need to go!'

This seems to shake Ben out of whatever state he was in, and he turns to Claire and nods. 'I'll call the pediatric unit and tell them we're on our way,' he says. 'It will all be OK, I promise.'

But even I can't miss the tremble in his voice.

I make sure to stay well out of the way as Ben and Claire tear around the house, flinging coats on over their nightwear and throwing things into a bag, and then Ben scoops Emily up, wraps her in a blanket and carries her downstairs and out to the car, whispering comforting words to her as they go. Outside, the sun is just coming up, turning the clouds gold and sending vivid red and purple streaks shooting across the horizon. I've never seen the sky look like this before, like it's blazing with fire, and I suddenly feel sure it's a sign that Emily will be OK because surely nothing bad could happen on such a beautiful day?

Ben has already started the car while Claire is locking up, and I hover by the front door, hoping she might let me stay outside so at least Lady can keep me company while I wait for news, but instead when Claire sees me she hesitates for a split second and then, to my astonishment, picks me up, grabbing Emily's red woolly scarf from the hatstand and wrapping it around me as we rush out the front door. As we hurry to the car, she drops a kiss on my fur.

'Thank you, Teddy,' she whispers. 'Thank you so much. You really are the most remarkable dog.'

I'm half-expecting Ben to complain as Claire drops me in the front passenger seat before climbing into the back to be with Emily, but he actually says to me, 'Good boy, Teddy.'

There isn't much talking during the drive. Claire occasionally murmurs some soothing words to Emily, who is still in that unnerving state of being asleep and awake at the same time, while Ben stays silent, his eyes fixed on the road ahead, although I can see just how worried he is. He's driving quite fast and I have to brace myself against the seat when we go round corners to stop myself flying off, but there aren't many other cars on the main road, probably because most people are still in bed, so we arrive at the hospital very quickly.

I'd heard quite a lot of talk about it while staying at Glebe Cottage, but I had no idea just how big the hospital would be. It is an enormous building, even bigger than the ones I had seen in the city, surrounded by rows and rows of cars that stretch as far as I can see. *Goodness*, I think as Ben tries to find a place to park the car, *there must be an awful lot of sick people around here!* With Ben carrying Emily and Claire holding me under her arm, we run up to the big glass doors, where we are met by a group of people who appear to be waiting for us. One of them – a stern-looking man wearing glasses – talks to Ben and Claire in an urgent sort of way, while other people dressed in blue uniforms put Emily onto a bed with wheels and race off with her. We follow, Ben and Claire still talking to the glasses-wearing man as we go. Perhaps this is the Dr Patterson that they mentioned the other day? We hurry along wide white corridors lined with doors, through which I get glimpses of yet more doors and more rooms, and I feel relieved that I'm still tucked under Claire's arm, as I imagine I'd get hopelessly lost if I had to find my own way out of here. As we go, we pass lots of other people in blue uniforms, who all seem very focused and serious, and I get the impression that Emily will be very well looked after here, which makes me feel a little bit less worried, although Claire clearly isn't reassured. Her heart is beating so fast that I can feel it pounding in her chest like a tiny, trapped animal struggling to be free, while her breath is coming in short, fearful gasps. I think back to that time in the kitchen when she told me about Emily being taken to hospital: she could barely talk about her memories of that dreadful time without crying, so goodness knows how hard this is for her. I nuzzle her hand in the hope of comforting her, but I don't think she even notices.

Now Emily is being wheeled away through another set of double doors, but this time we don't go with her. As the doors close behind her I look up at Claire and give a woof of encouragement: *Quick, we need to keep going or we'll lose her!* But then I see that Ben and the doctor have stopped too, and now he's leading us back up the corridor away from Emily and into a small windowless room which smells of fear and is empty apart from a few chairs and a withered pot-plant. The doctor tells Ben and Claire that he will return as soon as he has any further information, and then he leaves us alone. After the chaos and urgency of the past few hours suddenly all is silent and still. Claire collapses onto a chair, still holding me, and begins to cry. Ben quickly comes over to us, takes me out of her arms and places me gently on the floor and then wraps her in a hug.

'Shhh, don't cry, love. Emily's in the best possible hands. The team know exactly what they're dealing with this time, so she'll be getting all the help she needs, OK?'

Claire looks up at him, tears streaming down her face. 'I'm just so scared, Ben. Why is this happening again? I thought Emily was meant to be getting better . . .'

'She *is* getting better, but remember that Dr Patterson warned us that patients with chronic meningitis can occasionally suffer a relapse. We did know there was a chance this could happen.' Ben wipes a tear from Claire's cheek. 'But our little girl is a fighter, you know that. She's beaten this once and she'll do it again.'

'But it's just so unfair!' sobs Claire. 'She's still so tiny. Hasn't she been through enough?'

At this Ben's outwardly strong manner – which I've been finding so comforting – suddenly seems to waver: he lets his head fall, and I think I notice a tear in his eye. Seeing how worried he is beneath his brave face sends panic flooding through me again, but then he takes a deep breath, regains that reassuring sense of determination and pulls Claire closer to him.

'She's going to get through this,' he says firmly. 'We just need to stay strong for her, OK?'

They stay like this for a while, their arms around each other, until Claire's sobs subside into the occasional sniffle. I am desperate to join in with the hug too, as my insides are quivering with fear and confusion, but it seems like such a private moment I feel it's better not to intrude, so instead I curl up under one of the chairs, knowing there's nothing more that I can do to help. Now that I'm lying down I'm hit by a wave of tiredness; so much has happened since I woke up in

Emily's bed at first light that it feels like a whole day has passed. I'm still wearing the red scarf that Claire wrapped around me as we left, and its cosy warmth and the trace of Emily's scent comforts me as I drift off to sleep.

I don't know how much later in the day it is when I wake up to discover that I am on my own. Ben and Claire have disappeared, and the door to the little room is shut. There is a bowl of water sitting nearby on the floor though, so I clearly haven't been forgotten. I pad around the room, hoping to discover some clue as to where they've gone and how soon they might be back, but apart from their abandoned coats there's no trace of them at all, and as there aren't any windows in the room it's impossible to tell whether it's morning or afternoon.

I sit down in front of the door and whimper, desperate to know how Emily is doing. I know this place is enormous, but if I could somehow get out of this room and through the double doors where I last saw her being taken, perhaps I'd be able find her. Even if I did get lost, surely that would be preferable to just sitting here without a clue to what's going on?

Frustrated at my predicament, I push against the door with my head, and to my surprise I feel it yield slightly. With a surge of excitement, I try again, pushing harder this time and managing to get it open a crack, but the door is heavy and closes again before I can get out. *Come on, Teddy, you can do this!* Gathering all my strength, I give it an almighty shove, and this time I open it wide enough to wriggle through.

I find myself back on the busy corridor again, people bustling past in both directions. From what I remember, the doors through which Emily disappeared are straight down there and around the corner – yes, I definitely remember passing that row of chairs, because there'd been a little boy about Emily's age sitting there who smiled at me – so that's the direction I need to go. I set off, hiding in the shadows when people wearing the blue or white uniforms hurry past, who I now know from listening to Ben and Claire's conversation are nurses and doctors, although I feel sure that someone will stop me. After all, I've not seen any other dogs in here, especially not ones wearing bright red scarves. Yet everyone seems too busy or absorbed in their own problems to worry about me; in fact, the only person who notices me is a very old lady with hair the same colour as my fur, who is sitting on her own on the row of chairs where the boy was before, her hands resting in front of her on a stick. She breaks into a delighted smile as I go past.

'My, what a handsome boy you are!' She holds out her hand, and I bounce over to her, snuffling at her trembling fingers and wagging my tail, pleased to be making her smile. 'And I do like your scarf – you look most festive,' she says, then digs in her bag and pulls out a rich tea biscuit. 'Here, would you like one of these?'

Would I ever! I suddenly realise that I haven't eaten anything since last night. I've been so worried about Emily that I didn't even notice how hungry I am. Much to the old lady's delight, I gobble it down, showing my approval by licking my lips and scampering in a circle. She gives me another one, I let her stroke me for a little while longer, and then I give my new friend a goodbye yip and head off.

As I disappear around the corner, I hear the old lady saying, 'Anne, did you see that lovely puppy?'

'Are you quite sure, Mum?' It sounds like a younger

woman speaking. 'I don't think they allow dogs in here. Perhaps you were mistaken . . .'

I think about heading back to prove to the woman that her mother was right, but I really shouldn't get distracted. I need to focus on finding Emily.

I've now reached the double doors where I last saw her, but when I try to nudge them open it's obvious that they are far too heavy for me to move by myself, so I hide under a nearby trolley and wait for someone else to open them for me.

An opportunity comes almost immediately. Another of those beds on wheels is fast approaching, accompanied on either side by nurses, and as they push it through the doors I manage to slip in after them. Success!

I suppose it was too much to hope for that Emily would be waiting for me on the other side of the doors. Sure enough, I find myself in another wide windowless corridor, just as vast and daunting as the one before, stretching off into the distance with yet more doors leading off it and no clue as to where Emily might be found. There's a good chance she must be through one of these side doors, but which one should I pick? My sense of smell, which is usually so keen, is all but useless here, thanks to an overpowering chemical stench that lingers in the air, smothering any subtler scents and irritating the back of my throat. It reminds me of Shirley: she was forever washing the marble floors with something similar.

Without the help of my nose to guide me, my only choice is to check the rooms one at a time until I find Emily, which will take ages because – as I quickly find out – I can't open any of these doors on my own either. Then just along the corridor, one of the side doors swings open; well, I guess this is as good a place to begin as any. Taking my chance, I dive in, the rapidly unravelling scarf trailing behind me.

I find myself in an airy room, at the far end of which I'm relieved to get a glimpse of the outside world through a large window. Judging by the light, it must be early afternoon, which means I was asleep for quite a few hours. This realisation brings with it another jolt of fear: *What's been happening to Emily while I slept?* I need to find her.

There are beds down both sides of the room, a few of which have people in them, but I can tell from a quick glance that Emily isn't in here as they're all adults. My disappointment is rapidly replaced with embarrassment at intruding into these people's bedroom, especially as some of them appear to be asleep, and I'm just turning to leave when the door flies open and a nurse rushes into the room wheeling some sort of machine, and I only just manage to leap out of the way before getting hit. With a whimper, I manage to scamper out into the corridor before the door clicks shut. *Phew, that was a bit too close for comfort* . . .

Just as I'm pausing for a moment to catch my breath, I hear a shout: 'Hey, there are no dogs allowed in here!' Instantly on the alert, I turn towards the direction the voice came from to see a man hurrying down the corridor towards me. He looks surprised and rather cross, and he's moving pretty fast for a man of his advanced years. If he catches up with me then goodness only knows what will happen to me, as I don't have a collar with an address tag on it, so he won't know who I belong to; in fact, I might even get sent to those council kennels!

Spurred into action by this terrible thought, I turn and run as fast as I can in the opposite direction. Now that I've been spotted there's no point trying to keep myself hidden any more, so I race along the middle of the corridor where there are fewer things to bash into, but the flapping scarf keeps getting under my paws and I frequently stumble over it. People turn to watch as I race pass, pointing and laughing, and I feel fleetingly pleased to be brightening up their day before remembering about the kennels and the prospect of never seeing Emily again, which makes me run even faster.

Then behind me I hear a female voice raised in anger – 'Oi, watch where you're going!' – and I glance back to see sheets of paper fluttering through the air and a woman scrabbling around trying to catch them all. My pursuer stops for a moment to gabble his apologies but is quickly back on my tail.

With the man rapidly gaining on me, I career around a corner and by some wonderful doggy miracle I see a nearby door drifting shut, so with a final spurt of energy I scamper inside just as it closes – narrowly avoiding getting my scarf trapped in the process – and bolt under a desk. With my heart hammering in my chest I stay hidden in the cramped space, staying as quiet as I can, at any moment expecting the door to fly open and the man to burst in and find me, but the seconds tick past and he doesn't appear. Only when my breathing has slowed again and the fear that made my whole body go tense has almost faded away, do I feel confident enough that I've evaded capture to wriggle out from under the desk and explore my new surroundings.

I find myself in another room full of beds, similar in size and layout to the last one I was in, but with one big difference: whereas that room was rather plain-looking, the walls of this one are covered in cheery pictures of animals – including, I'm delighted to note, a puppy who looks rather like me. Over in the corner there are stacks of brightly coloured boxes filled with toys; Christmas decorations dangle from the ceiling and are festooned around each bed. It is by far the happiest-looking place I've come across in the whole hospital; in fact, it's all so colourful and dazzling that it takes me a moment to notice the very best thing of all: the room is full of children!

With a woof of glee, I bound up to the nearest bed, where a little boy has his arms stretched out towards me.

'Look, a puppy!' he cries, making the other children in the room sit up in their beds, craning to get a better look. With a flash of disappointment, I realise that Emily isn't among them, but I feel sure this is the right place to wait for her – and at least I can make some new friends in the meantime.

I hop my front paws up on the little boy's bed and let him stroke me, thrilled to see the happiness in his face. I remember Emily telling me how bored she was during her long stay in hospital. Perhaps these children have been here a long time too, in which case I should try my very best to cheer them up. Encouraged by their smiles, I dance around the room, revelling in the attention and the children's obvious delight. It's all so thrilling that I forget about the scarf I'm still wearing and, as I scamper between the beds, I get tangled up and fall jaws over paws, but that just makes the children laugh more, so I get up and do it again, sliding across the polished floor, my paws scrabbling in the air.

Then at the end of the room I notice a little girl, a bit younger than Emily at a guess, who is lying quietly in bed. She is smiling at me, but as I approach I can see how pale she is.

'Hello, Puppy,' she says in a voice little more than a whisper. 'Can I have a cuddle?'

I jump straight up, and it fleetingly crosses my mind that hospital beds are probably doggy no-go zones, but as I snuggle up with the little girl and she buries her face in my fur, just like Emily likes to do, the rules don't seem at all important.

We stay snuggled up together for a while as the little girl (whose name is Sophie, she tells me) chatters away, and I'm quite happy with her, but then a ball bounces towards us and I look up to see a boy kneeling on a nearby bed looking over at me expectantly.

I glance round at Sophie, who smiles and gives me a little shove as if to say, 'Well, what are you waiting for?' but before I go I wriggle out of the scarf – it's almost unwound by now anyway – pick it up in my jaws and drape it over her as best I can.

'Thank you,' she says, laughing in surprise.

'Come on, Puppy,' calls the boy who threw the ball, bouncing on his bed in anticipation. 'Fetch!'

Now, fetch I can *definitely* do. After giving Sophie one last nuzzle I leap off the bed, scoop up the ball in my jaws and return it to the boy as the other children clap and cheer. It's so much easier getting around now I don't have the scarf to slow me down. He throws it again, and this time, after scampering to retrieve it, I take it to one of the other beds for another of the children to have a turn. Back and forth I run, barking with excitement and slipping on the floor amid more laughter, and we're all having such fun that I don't notice the door opening.

'What on earth is going on in here?' says a horrified voice, sending me skidding to a halt. 'And who is *that*?'

I spin round to see a nurse, her hands on her hips, glaring at me. Frozen, I wonder if I should try to make a run for it, but then I realise that the door has already closed behind her. There's no way out.

'He's our new friend,' says the boy in the first bed I visited.

'We're playing with him,' a girl pipes up. 'Isn't he cute?'

'Can we keep him?' another one asks.

'We had a cuddle *and* he gave me his scarf,' says Sophie.

'Watch this,' says an older girl, and she throws the ball for me. 'Puppy, fetch!'

I glance at the nurse, whose expression is somewhere between surprised and angry, and stay where I am, too frightened to chase the ball. *That's it*, I think, I'm definitely going to be taken to the kennels, and I haven't even had a chance to find Emily! But after a moment, the nurse's face softens.

'Well go on then,' she says to me, nodding towards the ball. 'Aren't you going to show me what you can do?'

Still nervous that I might be in trouble, I scuttle over to fetch the ball and am about to return it to the girl who threw it when I have second thoughts, and instead gingerly creep up to the nurse, dropping it at her feet as a way of saying sorry.

To my relief, she breaks into a smile. 'What a clever boy,' she says, crouching down to give me a stroke. 'Well, I don't suppose it will matter that much if you stay here and play for a little while. I'm sure whoever you belong to can't be that far away.'

And with that she rolls the ball along the floor for me again, and as I scamper after it, woofing with glee, I hear her say, 'Just keep the noise down a bit, OK?'

A little while later I'm cuddled up with Sophie while

she sleeps when I hear the nurse, who is talking on the phone, mention something about 'a dog on the ward'. My ears instantly prick up. 'Yes, I was surprised too,' she is saying, making me worry all over again that I might be packed off to the kennels after all. Oh my goodness, perhaps she's even talking to that angry man who chased me earlier! I raise my head and listen as carefully as I can, but although the phone is still pressed to the nurse's ear she doesn't really say anything for a while, just the occasional 'Yes' or 'Hmmm,' and then she says, 'Ah, OK, I'll make sure he stays here until then,' and puts the phone down. At that moment she glances in my direction, sees me looking at her and smiles, before turning her attention back to the papers on her desk. Well, at least I don't seem to be in trouble, but time is ticking on – the daylight is already fading outside – and, as Emily still hasn't appeared, I need to resume my search for her. But how am I going to get away if the nurse has been told to keep me here?

From my vantage point on Sophie's bed I keep my eye on the nurse, who is now busy attending to one of the other children, then as luck would have it, she pulls a curtain around the bed and disappears inside. *Here's my chance!* Moving cautiously so as not to wake Sophie, I hop off the bed and make my way to the front desk, wriggling under it into my previous hiding place, from where I have a clear view of my escape route to the door.

Minutes pass; to my growing frustration nobody comes in or out. I hear footsteps returning to the desk and the nurse sits down, but I'm well hidden under here, if uncomfortably squashed and a bit dusty. I'm just wondering whether it's actually going to be possible for me to slip out unnoticed with the nurse sitting there when the door buzzer sounds. Well, it looks like I'm about to find out. There's a click as the nurse presses a button to let the visitor in. Here we go . . . *Now!*

With a surge of energy, I burst out from under the desk and run full pelt towards the opening door. I'm so focused on escape that I have no idea whether or not I've been seen, and I'm very nearly at the door and anticipating freedom when I hear someone say, 'Hey, not so fast, Teddy!' Although the familiar voice stops my paws mid-run, I'm going at such a lick that the rest of me keeps going, and I somersault across the floor, ending up in a heap at a man's feet. I look up to be greeted by Ben.

I scrabble to my feet, jumping up and covering his hands with ecstatic licks, but his appearance does little to soothe my worries over Emily. Still in the tatty T-shirt he threw on this morning, there is stubbly hair covering his chin and his eyes tell of heartache and hopelessness. He smiles as he reaches down to pick me up, ruffling my fur and clasping me to him with real affection, but I can sense that something is terribly wrong.

'Does this little guy belong to you, then?' asks the nurse, coming over to us.

'He does,' says Ben. 'I hope he wasn't too much trouble.'

'Not at all, the children loved having him here. What's his name?'

They talk for a little while longer, but I can tell Ben is keen to get going – as am I – and when there's a pause in the conversation he says, 'Well, thank you so much for looking after him, but I should get us both home now.'

As we leave, the children wave goodbye and blow kisses, asking me to come and visit again soon, but instead of being happy to be going back to Glebe Cottage all I can think is, *Where are Claire and Emily? And why aren't they coming home with us?*

As we make our way along the maze of corridors, my panic mounting with every step Ben takes, it suddenly occurs to me they're probably waiting for us in the car. Yes, of course, that must be it! Relief floods through me as I picture Emily sitting in the back seat, holding out her hands to give me a cuddle. Perhaps I'll even be allowed to sit on her lap on the way home . . .

Once we get outside into the chilly dusk air I begin wriggling in Ben's arms, desperate to get to Emily, but as we approach the car my excitement abruptly turns to dismay. She isn't there. Neither of them are.

I get the feeling both of us are thinking about that empty seat in the back as we get in – me in the front next to Ben – to begin the drive home. Ben turns the radio on, but when jolly Christmas music blares out he immediately reaches over to switch it off.

'Sorry, Ted, I'm not really in the mood,' he says apologetically as we turn out of the hospital car park.

Me neither, I think to myself.

'So, it's just you and me tonight, buddy,' he goes on.

'Claire won't leave Emily on her own, but she insisted that I come home. I didn't want to leave them, but I guess one of us should get some sleep . . .' His voice has the same defeated air as the rest of him, but now he puts on a brighter tone. 'Besides, I'm not sure the doctors would be very happy with you spending the night in hospital, even though you were obviously quite a hit on the children's ward.' As we wait at a junction, he smiles and reaches over to scratch under my chin.

In any other circumstances I would be thrilled at hearing the warmth in Ben's voice and seeing the fondness in his eyes, but all I can think about is Emily. I woof at Ben, hoping he might understand and tell me what's happened to her.

He glances at me. 'Are you hungry, boy? Don't worry, I'll get your tea as soon we get home. Claire says there's a bit of cold roast lamb in the fridge you can have. Only the best for the hero of the hour, eh?'

But even the prospect of dining on roast lamb does little to dent my worries. I bark again, more sharply this time.

Ben looks at me quizzically. 'Teddy? What's wrong? It's OK, we're nearly home.'

Oh, this is no good. I need to find some way of making him understand. I look round the car, searching for something that might help get my message across – some sort of clue that I could give to Ben – and my eyes fall on Cyril, Emily's cuddly penguin, who is lying on the back seat. Before Ben can stop me, I jump into the back, snatch up Cyril in my jaws and then drop him in his lap, sitting back with my head cocked to one side and my tail wagging hopefully.

Ben looks like he's about to tell me off for distracting him from driving, but then he sees the penguin and his lip trembles like he's about to cry. He regains his composure though, and after a moment he glances at me with a sad smile. 'Are you missing Emily, boy? Yes, me too. But she can't come home today, Ted, she's still too poorly. They're keeping her in the HDU – that's the high dependency unit – and we're just hoping by some miracle that the doctors will let her go tomorrow so that she's back home for Christmas, although right now it doesn't seem likely. Her temperature shot up so dramatically this morning that the doctors have to be careful.'

We're now pulling into the driveway of Glebe

Cottage. Ben turns off the engine, but he doesn't make any move to get out.

'The good news though,' he goes on, 'is that Dr Patterson believes she's getting stronger every day, despite this setback, so that's fantastic, isn't it?' He looks at me hopefully and I find myself wishing more than ever that I could speak human so I could reassure him. 'It's just . . . seeing her back in hospital again, unconscious and so horribly pale, it brought back all those terrible memories of the last time, when the doctors warned us she might . . . well, might not pull through. As a father, seeing your child suffering like that and not being able to do a thing to make it better . . .' He tails off, staring into the darkness outside the car, his face etched with helplessness, then looks back at me. 'D'you know, Teddy, when we were sitting in hospital first thing this morning, waiting for news on Emily's condition, I found myself wishing desperately that my parents were still alive. It's the weirdest thing. They passed away some time ago, and although I miss them, it's not like there's a huge hole in my life, but at that moment I would have given anything for my mum to give me a hug and tell me Emily would be OK. I needed to stay strong for Claire, but all I wanted to do was to curl up on the floor and cry, and it felt like only my mum or dad could stop the feelings of fear and utter helplessness.'

Ben chokes on the last word, and though his hand quickly flies up to whisk it away, I see a tear trickle down his cheek. Without a second thought I jump onto his lap – not that easy, as the steering wheel is in the way – and cover his face with enthusiastic licks. It's something I would do without hesitation to Emily or even Claire, but I've never felt confident enough about Ben's feelings towards me for such an overt display of doggy affection. He needs me now, though, I'm sure of that; he might not have his mum to give him a hug and tell him everything will be OK, but I can. True, I'm not a doctor, but I know how much of a fighter Emily is and have sensed how strong she is at heart, and I've seen just how much love there is between Claire and Ben. This family will be fine, I'm sure of it; I just need to make Ben believe that.

He laughs, wiping his face, then gently pushes me away. 'Hey, enough with the kisses, Teddy!' But as I sit back on the front passenger seat, wagging my tail, he leans over to pick me up, then presses his cheek to my fur. 'Thank you,' he says softly. He holds me out in front of him, so that we're looking right into each other's eyes. 'Claire's right, you know,' he says. 'You really are the most remarkable dog.'

When we get into the house, Ben goes straight to the kitchen to make my tea, as promised, and while I gobble down the very tasty leftover lamb, suddenly feeling ravenous, he pours himself a large glass of red liquid from a bottle of the sort that I've often seen in their kitchen – and in Richard and Veronica's too.

'I suppose I should probably eat something as well,' says Ben, opening the fridge. He bends down and pokes around inside, picking stuff up, looking at labels, sniffing things and putting them back again, before taking them out again for another look. I've never seen Ben do much cooking and he's clearly confused. Still crouched in front of the fridge, he looks round at me.

'Cheese on toast it is then,' he says, forcing a smile.

But as Ben moves around the kitchen preparing his meal, his sloping shoulders and the lines creasing his face make his pain and worry all too obvious. He puts his food in the Aga and then heads for the living room – with me tagging along, just to make sure he's OK –

where he slumps onto the sofa and takes a long gulp of his red drink. He stares at the Christmas tree for a moment, perhaps thinking about Emily, then retrieves his phone from his pocket and fiddles with it in that odd way that humans like to do. I stay sitting at his feet, looking up at him.

'No news from the hospital,' he says after a moment. Then he shakes his head as if trying to dislodge a painful memory, his face clouded again. 'Emily looked so tiny in that bed, like a doll. And so fragile . . . You wouldn't believe what a live wire she used to be, Teddy. Here, let me find something . . .' He turns his attention back to his phone. 'Yes, here it is.' As he watches the screen, his face lights up. 'I can't believe this video was taken last summer,' he says in wonder. 'We went to France on holiday for two weeks, and at the end of every day we had to pull Emily out of the pool, she loved it so much. She had so much energy! Oh, and I filmed this one at her fifth birthday party. Emily wanted a princess theme, but on the day she insisted on going as a one-legged pirate called Bob.' He chuckles to himself, taking another swig from his glass, which is nearly empty now. 'And look, here's Claire with the birthday cake! She spent hours making that cake in the shape of a princess, just like Emily wanted, then minutes before the party begined she had to ice an eyepatch on it.' He keeps watching, entranced. 'God, Claire looks stunning in that dress. And so happy, like she doesn't have a care in the world. I haven't seen her look like that for a while.' He glances towards me. 'You should have seen her on our wedding day, Ted, she was so beautiful. I really am a very lucky man . . .'

Just then I get a waft of an acrid smell coming from the kitchen, and trot over to the doorway to investigate. To my horror, a wisp of black smoke is seeping out of the Aga. *Oh no, Ben's dinner!* I scamper back to the sofa, barking to alert him.

'Oh, so you agree, do you?' He laughs, completely misreading my increasingly urgent woofs. 'Don't worry; I know. Claire is an amazing woman. You know what I'm going to do, Teddy? When Christmas is out of the way I'm going to book a babysitter and take her out for a really nice dinner, somewhere posh so we can get all dressed up.' I scrabble at his leg, but he just ruffles my head. 'It's a good idea, isn't it? I don't think I've taken her out on a date since Emily got ill – it just never seemed the right time – but it's the very least she deserves after everything she's done for this family. She's been incredible, looking after Emily and supporting me while I tried to get the garden design business off the ground, while I . . . I don't think I've coped very well. I certainly haven't always been the best husband. But from now on, well, that's all going to change.' Then he finally seems to notice my panic. 'Teddy, what on earth's wrong?' His head flicks towards the kitchen. 'Oh my God, the cheese on toast!'

He leaps up and rushes into the kitchen, from where I hear banging and clattering, then as I follow him in he turns to face me holding out something charred and smoking.

'I'll just have some cereal' He shrugs. 'I wasn't that hungry anyway.'

Later that evening I'm snuggled up on Ben's lap as he sits watching a film on television. Martha is lying on the sofa next to us with her tail wrapped around her body; she appeared a little while ago, slipping in through her cat flap and then sitting on the doormat, busying

herself with washing a paw as if deciding whether or
not to pay us any attention, before padding over and
jumping up to join us, although she pointedly posi-
tioned herself as far from me as possible.

She looks like she's asleep, but every now and then
I'll catch her green-yellow eyes on me, perhaps making
sure that I'm not about to pounce on her. Still, the idea
that Martha might deign to share a sofa with me was
unthinkable even a day ago, and I'm overjoyed that
she's apparently accepted me at Glebe Cottage. And
it's not just Martha who seems to have had a change
of heart about my presence tonight.

'Where did you come from, Teddy?' Ben asked
me earlier as he settled back on the sofa after dinner.
'Emily reckons Father Christmas left you on the doorstep, and who knows, perhaps she's right. It certainly
feels – and I've probably had too much wine – but
it almost it feels like you were brought to us for a
reason. It's like you're looking out for us, and judging
by what happened this morning – and just now with
the cheese on toast – God knows we need it!' And
then he picked me up and put me on his lap. 'You
know, all this time I've been worried you'll be too

much work, but I think perhaps you're the very thing this family was missing.'

Even though Emily's absence still hung over us like a dark cloud, for the first time since leaving my mum and littermates I finally felt that blissful sense of peace and happiness that comes with being part of a loving family.

❄ *Christmas Eve* ❄

I'm dozing in the garden, the sun warming my fur, when a fly begins buzzing around somewhere nearby. It's making such a racket that I'm sure it must be one of those horribly fat, shiny ones. If I could only see where it is, I might be able to snap at it, or swat it with my paw. Anything to stop that infuriating noi—

'Hello? Claire?'

My eyes snap open and I realise that, rather than being outside, I'm still on Ben's lap, and that buzzing wasn't a fly after all, but his phone, which he now has pressed to his ear. I jump off his lap and give myself a shake, and it's only then that I realise how bright the room is, and I look towards the window to discover light pouring in. *Goodness, we must have slept on the sofa all night!* I glance at the window again; the daylight seems to have a strange quality – it's somehow brighter and whiter than usual – but I can't worry about that now. If Ben's talking to Claire I need to focus on the conversation to get some news on Emily.

'But what did Dr Patterson say?' he is asking. 'Did he seem concerned?'

He listens in silence for a while, his expression giving little away, and I wish I could hear what Claire is saying to him.

'OK.' He nods. 'I see. I'll be there as quickly as I can. Oh, and Claire? I love you.'

He puts the phone back in his pocket, runs a hand through his unruly hair, and then notices me watching him.

'Ted, we're going back to the hospital, but I need to grab a shower first. Why don't you have a run around outside and then I'll make you some breakfast?'

But what about Emily? I'm desperate to know how she is this morning, but Ben is clearly focused on getting up and out of the house as quickly as possible, which is perfectly understandable. Yet when he opens the front door, the sight that greets us stops both of us in our tracks. No wonder the light looked so different: the whole world has turned a brilliant, blinding white. A dazzling shroud of snow covers everything, even balancing along the slenderest branches of the leafless trees, and still more is falling, the plump flakes tumbling so thickly that it looks like there's more snow than sky. Almost as striking as the whiteness is the complete stillness; it's as if nature has been stunned into silence. It's a magical sight, but there's so much snow coming down – and so fast – that I wonder if it will *ever* stop; perhaps that's the reason Ben's suddenly looking so worried? He watches the snow for a moment longer, then mutters, 'We've got to get going,' before hurrying back into the house.

It's only after we've had breakfast and Ben is dressed and ready to go that I discover the reason for his concern: the car is covered in snow, as is the driveway *and* the road. How on earth are we going to get to the hospital?

'OK, Teddy,' says Ben, disappearing into the garage and emerging armed with a spade. 'Are you ready to do some digging?'

Am I ever! We set to work, Ben with the spade and me scrabbling with my paws, and luckily the snow is so light and fluffy that it doesn't take long for us to make good progress. Apart from chewing, I think that digging is probably my favourite pastime, and I'm so enjoying myself – all the more so because I'm actually being useful – that I keep scrabbling away even after I've reached the driveway, peppering the bank of cleared snow with a shower of gravel.

'I think that's enough there, Teddy,' calls Ben. 'Here, come and help me with this bit.'

Ben keeps the car's engine running while we're working, and by the time we've finished clearing a pathway along the drive I'm amazed to notice that the snow on the car's front and back windows has simply melted away like magic. Ben chucks his spade to one side, in too much of a rush to return it to the garage, and climbs in the car.

'Come on, boy, jump in,' he calls, opening the passenger door for me. I hop in next to him and we roll smoothly towards the end of the driveway, where we come to a halt.

So what now? It's clear that no other cars have

attempted to get down the lane, as the snow lies undisturbed here in a perfectly smooth blanket. Perhaps we should walk to the hospital instead? It would take a while, but I really don't fancy trying to drive down a slippery, snow-covered hill. I remember all too clearly the night that I first came to Glebe Cottage (it was just a few days ago, but feels like another lifetime now) and the struggle I had to haul myself up the snowy, sloping garden without sliding to the bottom. I glance at Ben, assuming that he must have some sort of plan, but he is just watching the road as if waiting for something to happen. We've been sitting there for a few minutes when I hear a far-off rumble that grows into a roar, and then rolling down the lane towards us comes that huge vehicle with the gigantic wheels that we ran into the other day – a tractor, I think Ben called it.

As it trundles past our drive, Ben leans his head out of the window and calls, 'Cheers, Dave. I owe you one!'

The man driving the tractor smiles at us and touches his hat in greeting, and it's only now that I notice that he is pulling a machine cutting a channel through the snow. I bark with excitement; we can do this!

'Now, let's just hope the ploughs have been out on

the main road,' mutters Ben as he steers the car out of the drive and heads gingerly down the lane behind the tractor.

Thankfully, there's been enough traffic on the bigger, busier roads to make them passable, and the drive is largely uneventful, but as we approach the hospital Ben's unflinching stare and the way he's gripping the steering wheel reveal just how tense he is. I'm hoping that it's just the stress of driving in the snow, but I can't help worrying that perhaps it's because Emily's condition has worsened overnight, and when we finally arrive at the hospital his haste to get inside does little to soothe my fears. Carrying me in his arms, Ben hurries up to the entrance and is now almost running along the corridors, panting with the exertion, and although I tell myself that it's just because he's keen to see Claire and Emily, what if it's because something terrible has happened? I want to be strong for Ben, so I'm just glad that his heavy breathing drowns out my anxious whimpers.

Then we approach a familiar-looking door, and as I realise we're back at the children's ward I feel a jumble of emotions: happiness at seeing my new friends again, disappointment at the thought that Ben might leave me here while he goes to see Emily without me, and most fervent of all, hope that Emily is actually here now.

The same nurse lets us in, but when I frantically scan the beds, searching for that familiar pale-gold head, I can't see her. My heart plummets to my paws; that must mean that she's still in the special care unit Ben mentioned, which means there's no way she'll be coming home with us today. Oh, this is terrible. Emily has been so excited about Christmas and now she's going to have to spend it in hospital! Claire and Ben will be heartbroken too. Even worse, perhaps this means that Emily's more poorly than I thought – and I was *so* sure she was going to beat this . . .

'Teddy!'

My head swings round in the direction of her voice and then I see her, not only here but up and kneeling on a striped rug next to Sophie and a pile of toys! She's still in her dressing gown, but with a flush of colour on her cheeks and a huge smile on her face. She holds out her arms to me, and with a yip of pure joy I jump out of Ben's arms, landing in a furry heap by his feet, then pick myself up and race over to where she's sitting, my paws skidding on the slippery floor in my hurry to get to her.

'I've missed you so much, Teddy.' She giggles as I cover her in ecstatic licks and jump up to put my paws around her neck in a doggy cuddle.

'It looks like someone's pleased to see you too, Ems.' I look up to see Claire sitting in a chair nearby and bounce over to say hello, my tail wagging so frantically it makes my whole body wiggle, and jump onto her lap.

Then Ben bends down and scoops Emily up, and although he holds her to him so tightly that his face is all but hidden by her hair, I'm sure I see tears springing in his eyes as he says softly, 'I love you so much, my gorgeous girl.'

They stay like that for a while, and then, still holding Emily, Ben comes over to where we're sitting and gathers Claire and me up into the hug too. Cocooned by their arms and familiar smell, I feel as safe and loved as back when I was a tiny puppy, curled up with my mum and siblings. It's a feeling that lingers even after Emily wriggles down out of their embrace and Claire puts me back on the floor.

'So Dr Patterson has said that Emily can come home

today,' says Claire, and although she looks weary her face is radiating happiness.

'He said I was as tough as old boots,' says Emily proudly. 'I am, aren't I, Daddy?'

'You certainly are, sweetheart. How are you feeling this morning?'

'Well, I had porridge for breakfast, which was lumpy and disgusting, and that made me feel worse, but then the nurse brought me a bacon sandwich, and when I finished that I felt so much better that I had another one.'

Claire and Ben exchange smiles.

'You're certainly looking better,' says Ben. 'So, how soon are we allowed to take you home?'

'Not yet, Daddy!' Emily suddenly looks panicked. 'Father Christmas is coming, and I can't miss him! Please can I stay a bit longer? Pleeeeease?'

Father Christmas is going to be here? Well this *is* interesting news. I've heard so much about this man, it would be wonderful to meet him, and it's as much to my relief as Emily's that Claire and Ben agree we can stay until he's visited.

While we wait, I play with Emily and the rest of the

children. It's a smaller group of us today, as some of my friends from yesterday have gone home, but no less enthusiastic. Sophie is particularly pleased to see me again, and I'm thrilled at how much livelier she is today, throwing the ball for me and whooping as I scamper after it. Emily has been in the next-door bed to her and they have already become good friends.

'Can we dress Teddy up in some of these doll's clothes?' Sophie asks her as they play together on her bed.

'No, he definitely wouldn't like that,' says Emily firmly, and I give her hand a grateful lick, the memory of that itchy pink jacket Veronica dressed me in still lurking in my mind.

Just then there's a loud bang on the door that makes us all look up.

'I wonder who that could be, children?' says the nurse at the front desk with a smile, as an excited murmur ripples through the room.

She opens the door, and the most astonishing-looking figure I've ever seen strides onto the ward and flings out his arms in greeting. He is dressed all in red with big black boots and is carrying a huge sack, but the most striking thing about him is the mass of white hair covering his face and peeking out from under his hat. I shrink behind Emily, suddenly scared. So this is Father Christmas then? I'm not sure exactly what I was expecting, but I thought he might look a little more . . . approachable.

'Ho ho ho! Merry Christmas, everyone!' His voice is so loud and booming it makes me jump, but it's full of warmth, plus the children certainly seem overjoyed to see him, which makes me feel a little less afraid. Still, I think I might go and sit with Ben and Claire, just to be on the safe side.

Father Christmas makes his way down the ward, stopping to talk to each of the children in turn, before reaching into his sack and handing them something. It's only as he gets nearer that I realise what he's got in the sack: presents!

Eventually, it's Emily's turn. Claire gets up from her chair so Father Christmas can sit there, then she joins Emily on her bed. I hop onto Ben's lap to get a better look.

'Hello there – you must be Emily,' says Father Christmas, and now I'm close to him I can see the kindness in his eyes.

Suddenly shy, Emily just nods, while Claire gives her hand a supportive squeeze.

'Now, I've heard that you've been a very good girl this year, is that right?'

Emily, now chewing nervously on her thumb, nods again.

'She certainly has,' says Claire. 'And very brave too.'

'I've had meningitis,' Emily pipes up, finally finding her voice.

'Well that doesn't sound at all nice,' says Father Christmas, 'but the doctors tell me you're feeling much better now.'

Emily breaks into a grin. 'I am. I had *two* bacon sandwiches this morning.'

Father Christmas laughs, holding his huge belly. 'That sounds like my kind of breakfast! Now, because you've been so good and so brave, I've brought you an early Christmas present. Would you like that?'

'Yes please!' says Emily, bouncing on the bed with excitement.

He reaches into his sack and hands her a package wrapped in paper covered in lots of little Christmas trees, which Emily quickly rips open. Inside, there is a doll with long hair exactly the same colour as hers.

'Thank you!' she says delightedly, clutching it to her.

'You're very welcome,' says Father Christmas, his eyes twinkling. Then to my surprise, he looks over at me. 'And who's this then?'

'His name's Teddy,' says Emily, busying herself with the doll. 'Would you like to stroke him?'

Before I have the chance to jump off his lap, Ben picks me up and carries me over to Father Christmas. I kick my legs a little in protest, not sure I'm ready to get *that* close to him, but as he holds me gently and scratches me under my chin in just the right spot, I begin to relax. I'm expecting Father Christmas to smell like gingerbread, which is the scent that I've come to associate with Christmas, but curiously what he actually smells of is coffee.

'Well now, Teddy, have you been a good boy this year?'

Have I been a good boy? Oh my goodness, I really don't know . . . There was the unfortunate incident with the mouse and the Christmas Tree for starters, which while it might have been an accident, certainly couldn't be classed as 'good'. Then there was the time I dug up Ben's flower bed – again, a complete mis-understanding, but one that didn't reflect at all well on me – and what about that morning when I ate the Christmas decorations off the tree and then chased Martha? I really didn't mean any harm, but I still caused a load of trouble, didn't I? All in all, I'm afraid that I haven't been very good at all, and I drop my head in shame at the thought of all the fuss and mess I've caused. I guess this means that I won't be getting a present after all . . .

But then to my surprise, I hear Ben say, 'Teddy's been a *very* good boy.'

'He's a wonderful dog,' says Claire, 'and we're very lucky to have him.'

Then she smiles at me, and any remaining worries I had over my future with the Woods vanish, swept aside by a wave of perfect happiness.

'Well then, I think I might have the perfect present for you.' Father Christmas smiles, puts me on the bed and rummages in the sack again, then holds out a small package.

I take it in my jaws and give it an experimental chew;

it makes a satisfyingly loud squeak. This is fantastic! I wag my thanks to him and then jump around the bed, squeaking as I go, puffed up with pride about my first ever Christmas present.

'You need to unwrap it first, silly.' Emily laughs.

Oh yes, of course! With her help, I tear off the paper and inside find a chewy toy in the shape of a woman's shoe. To my astonishment, it's virtually identical to the shoe of Veronica's that I chewed all those weeks ago, right down to the strappy bits and bright red sole. I look back at Father Christmas in amazement. Emily said he was magical, but surely he couldn't know about that?

'I thought you might like that, Teddy,' he says with a wink. 'Well Emily, I'd better get going now as I have an awful lot to do before tomorrow, but I'll see you again tonight. Not that you'll see me, of course!'

Then with a cheery wave and another booming 'Ho ho ho!' he moves on to the next bed.

'Right then, missy,' says Ben, turning to Emily with a smile. 'Are you ready to go home?'

❄ *Christmas Day* ❄

'Teddy? Teddy, wake up . . . Teddy!'

I open my eyes to discover Emily crouched down next to my potato-box bed, wearing her dressing gown and slippers. Although the kitchen is still quite dark, I can see that her face is alive with excitement.

'It's Christmas morning,' she says in a loud whisper. 'And Father Christmas has been!'

What, he's been here? Inside the house? Oh my goodness, I must have been fast asleep, as I usually wake up as soon as the front door opens. What a shame I missed him! I would have liked to see him again, not least to thank him properly for the fantastic squeaky shoe. I barely put it down yesterday.

So, after all the excitement and preparation, Christmas is finally here! I glance towards the window, half-expecting the world to look somehow different on this momentous day, but as far as I can make out in the dawn light the garden hasn't changed that much since yesterday.

'Come with me, Teddy,' says Emily, and she heads into the living room with me trotting behind. Even after her recent scare, it's wonderful to see how much stronger and steadier on her feet she is now compared to when I first arrived. Then she crouches down by the fireplace and beckons me over. 'Look, Teddy. Father Christmas has left sooty footprints from where he came down the chimney!'

Hang on a moment – Father Christmas got inside the house by coming down the chimney? With that great big tummy of his? Well, that *is* a surprise. I'd have thought the poor man would have got stuck.

'And he ate the mince pies I left for him,' Emily goes on, her voice squeaking with excitement. 'And the reindeers had the carrots!'

As the curtains are still closed, the living room is dark except for the twinkling lights on the Christmas tree, and their flickering glow gives the room such a magical look that suddenly the idea of Father Christmas managing to get down the chimney – sack, tummy and all – doesn't seem quite so unbelievable after all. And sure enough, just as Emily said, there is a scattering of large boot-shaped footprints in front of the fireplace. Well I never! I have a tentative sniff of the hearth, searching for traces of Father Christmas, but funnily enough the only person's scent that I can pick up is Ben's.

'Teddy, look at this!' Emily points to the giant red sock hanging over the fireplace, which is now bulging with presents, so many that some of the brightly wrapped packages are poking out of the top; not only that, but there is the most enormous gift I have ever seen, bigger even than Emily, propped up nearby.

'Do you know what that is, Teddy?' Emily is jumping up and down on the spot, just like I do when I'm excited. 'I think it's a bike!'

Although I remember her mentioning this before, I have no idea what a bike actually is. But Emily's enthusiasm is so infectious that I join in, barking and scampering in circles.

'Shhhhh, Teddy. Mummy and Daddy are still asleep!'

Emily glances upstairs, but all is still quiet. 'They've said that I have to wait until they're up to open my presents from Father Christmas, but I'm sure they won't mind if I open a little tiny one, will they?'

I give my quietest woof to let Emily know that I'm sure they wouldn't mind at all, and then sit back and watch as she stands on her tiptoes and reaches inside the sock, pulling out one of the packages.

With a delighted smile in my direction, she rips open the paper.

'Ooh, look. Lego!'

Whatever this is, it is clearly something that Emily wanted very much, and she sits on the floor, takes it out of the box and begins to play. It's not something that I can join in with, but I'm happy to sit by her side and watch.

A little while later I hear footsteps and look up to see Ben and Claire, still in their dressing gowns, coming downstairs. They both look tired, but the tense, worried look that so often haunts their eyes has vanished. I jump up to greet them with licks and snuffles, while they bend down to hug Emily, scooping her up into their arms. I get the impression that Ben and Claire would happily stay like that, but after a moment Emily disentangles herself from their embrace and points to the fireplace.

'Mummy! Daddy! Father Christmas has been – look!'

Claire gives a gasp. 'Oh my goodness, so he has!'

'And what on earth is that over there?' Ben points to the enormous present. 'Surely that's not for you too?'

'It is, Daddy, it really is! Look, it's got my name on it!' Emily's eyes are wide and dancing with delight. 'And I think it might be a *bike*!'

While Emily begins opening the rest of her presents, Claire lets me into the garden for my morning run. As soon as I get outside I can tell it's been snowing again, as my tracks from yesterday have been blurred by a sprinkling of white flakes, like a dusting of icing sugar, but the sun is now shining, making the snow sparkle in a perfectly Christmassy fashion. I bound down the garden, woofing with delight as I bowl along, sending a group of birds scattering up into the air with indignant squawks, their wings black against the world's whiteness. Perhaps it's because it's such a special day, but I'm suddenly filled with such an overwhelming, all-consuming happiness that I feel like I could almost fly myself. Actually . . . perhaps I *can* fly? I might not have wings, and I'm pretty sure Mum never said anything to us about dogs being able to fly, but Veronica was always making plans to fly somewhere or other – and if humans can do it, I'm quite sure that dogs can too. We're certainly better at running and jumping than humans, that's for sure.

My heart thumping with anticipation, I scamper back up the slope to make sure I can pick up enough speed to take off, and then I turn and race at full speed down the hill. Here we go . . . I spring upwards, my paws scrabbling at nothing but air, feeling a thrilling soaring sensation – then the next moment I'm up to my ears in snow. *Oh well.* I pick myself up, shaking the snow off my fur and ears and sneezing it out of my nose. Perhaps I wasn't doing it right. I'll ask Lady about it, she's sure to know.

Lady. It's only been two days since we last spoke, but at the thought of her I'm struck by a desperate longing to see my friend. I make my way through the snow to the gap in the fence where we meet for our chats, and peer cautiously into her garden in case grumpy Tobias is about, but there's no sign of her – and, as the snow has smothered the usual scent trails, I can't tell whether or not she's been around recently. Perhaps they've gone away for Christmas? My spirits fall a little at the thought, and I realise how much I've come to rely on her friendship.

I get back inside the cottage just in time to see Emily start tearing the paper off the enormous present. Martha has appeared since I've been outside and is sitting halfway up the stairs, watching what's going on.

When Emily discovers what's inside the present her eyes go very big and she gasps like it's the best thing she's ever seen.

'It *is* a bike! Father Christmas brought me a bike!'

She runs her hands admiringly over its sleek frame while her parents look on, smiling at each other. Ah, so that's what a bike is! I saw a lot of them in London, but this one is particularly fine-looking: shiny red with a white seat and silver streamers hanging from the handlebars. No wonder Emily looks so happy.

'Do you like it?' asks Claire, which strikes me as quite a funny thing to say because it's blindingly obvious that Emily adores it.

Sure enough: 'I love it,' she breathes, her cheeks

pink with pleasure. 'It's the best bike in the whole wide world.'

'When the weather improves, we'll go out and give it a try,' says Ben.

Then all of a sudden, Emily's grin fades. 'But am I going to be well enough?' she asks in a small voice, looking between her parents with fear in her eyes.

Ben puts his arms around her. 'Yes, you will.' He smiles. 'I know you will. You're as tough as old boots, remember?'

Breakfast is scrambled eggs – for all of us, even Martha and me. While Martha daintily picks at hers, taking tiny, elegant mouthfuls, I gobble down the silky, buttery curds in seconds, licking my lips to make sure I haven't missed a scrap. If you judged us by our eating habits, it's really no wonder that Ben and Claire thought I was to blame for the cake disaster! Thankfully though my misdemeanours now seem forgiven, as when Claire notices my licked-clean dish she spoons in more of the eggs.

'Happy Christmas, Teddy,' she says as I nuzzle her hand in gratitude.

Emily finishes her plateful and clatters her knife and

fork together. 'Mummy, when can we open the presents under the tree?'

'After lunch, like we always do, sweetheart. Now, we have to get on with preparing the lunch. Do you want to help?'

'Yes please!'

'OK then, missy,' says Ben, 'but let's go up and get you dressed first.'

While Ben and Emily disappear upstairs to get ready, Claire ties an apron over her dress and gets to work. The radio is on, filling the room with festive songs, while the occasional snowflake flutters past the window.

'I can't remember our last white Christmas,' murmurs Claire, stopping for a moment to look outside. 'It's so beautiful.'

She stands there for a moment, gazing entranced at the snowy scene, then crosses over to the fridge, and now it's my turn to stare in wonder as she brings out the most enormous chicken I have ever seen. It is absolutely gigantic, even bigger than I am; I had no idea chickens got this big! While Claire prepares the giant chicken for the Aga, humming along to the songs on the radio as she stuffs it with something delicious-smelling, I stand on my back legs to get a better look, my nose twitching impatiently.

Claire looks down at me and smiles. 'Don't worry, Teddy. There'll be plenty to go round, and lots of left-overs too. I wasn't expecting it to be quite this big!' Then she stands back, hands on hips and head on one side, and looks at the chicken. 'Hmmm . . . I just hope it fits in the oven.'

A little while later Ben and Emily come back down-stairs, both looking very festive. Emily is in a red dress, with her pale-gold hair tied up in a matching ribbon, while Ben is wearing a jumper with a huge picture of Father Christmas's face on the front, like something a child might wear. Claire bursts out laughing when she sees him.

'What do you think?' He grins. 'Pretty cool, right?'

'Where on earth did you find *that*?'

'I saw it in the charity shop in the village. I thought it would make you smile.'

'Well it certainly did,' says Claire, looking at him with love in her eyes, and he blows her a kiss.

'What can I do to help, Mummy?' asks Emily, clambering up and kneeling on one of the chairs around the table. 'I'll do anything except the sprouts. I'm not even *touching* the sprouts.'

'Why don't you help Daddy with the pigs in blankets,' says Claire, fishing around in the fridge and, to my disbelieving delight, putting a packet of sausages *and* a stack of streaky bacon rashers on the table. This is *all* for lunch? I won't need to eat for a week after this!

Ben helps Emily wrap bacon around the sausages, while Claire stands at the sink peeling potatoes. Their earthy smell reminds me of my cosy box-bed, but I'm not sure that they'll taste particularly nice. I think I'll just stick to the giant chicken and the bacon-covered sausages. That should be just about enough for me – oh, and perhaps one of those yummy-sounding mince pies too . . .

Thanks to the excitement of the morning (and our very early start), Emily begins to flag after helping in the kitchen for a while, so she goes for a nap on the sofa, and I join her for a blissful doze in front of the fire, dreaming of giant chickens dancing through a world made of bacon, with sausage trees. By the time

Claire wakes us up, the cottage is full of heavenly smells that make my mouth drool with anticipation.

'Lunchtime.' She smiles, helping Emily up from the sofa.

I follow them into the kitchen, and what a sight greets our eyes! The table is decorated with gold candles sitting in wreathes of red-berried holly; there are gold-trimmed plates, green napkins and special glasses that I've never seen before that catch the sunlight and sparkle like they're lit up from inside. And sitting in the middle of all this magnificence, perfectly bronzed and smelling like a dog's dream, is the stupendous giant chicken. My paws tingle, itching to get at it. If I wasn't a well-behaved dog I would take a flying leap onto that table and tuck straight in. But that's not the only delight: there's a bowl of those sausages wrapped in bacon, golden roast potatoes (which smell so good that I think I might have to try one or two after all), carrots and all sorts of other dishes of things I don't recognise but which look extremely tempting. Even the hated sprouts look quite tasty. There is so much food I can't imagine we'll eat even half of it.

As Claire helps Emily into her seat, Ben carves up the giant chicken and I sit at his feet, my tail wagging so fast it's a blur. The smell of the chicken transports me back to the first night that I came to Glebe Cottage, when I was led here by the same irresistible scent. I really couldn't have imagined then quite how wonderfully things would have turned out for me, a lost, homeless, puppy, but now here I am, part of a loving family with a wonderful home where I can stay for ever. Well, I *think* I'll be able to stay here for ever, even though Ben and Claire haven't said as much. They've certainly implied that's the case, although they haven't told me that for sure, have they? As I rack my brain, desperately trying to remember the lovely things Claire and Ben said about me being part of the family, a tiny doubt pops into my mind, but I push it away. *It will all be fine. I'm sure it will . . .*

Suddenly there's a frenzied scrabbling sound at the front door which interrupts my thoughts and makes us all jump. Ben looks at Claire quizzically; she shrugs in reply.

'I think there's somebody here,' says Emily. 'Ooh, perhaps Father Christmas is back again!'

Ben gets up and starts towards the front door. 'I don't think it'll be Father Christmas, sweetie, but I'll go and have a look . . .'

I hear the door opening, and then a split second later, in a blur of silky fur, snow and flying paws, Lady races into the room. She rushes straight up to me and covers me with kisses, her gorgeous black eyes wide with relief.

'Oh Teddy, you're here, thank goodness! I thought you might have been sent away!'

I bounce around her in delight, thrilled to see her, and out of the corner of my eye I catch Ben and Claire exchanging suprised smiles.

'Teddy's got a girlfriend!' cries Emily delightedly, watching our ecstatic reunion.

Lady touches my nose and then sits down, now back to her usual elegant self, and explains the reason for her impromptu visit.

'I hadn't picked up a trace of you in the garden since we last spoke, and I've been so frantic with worry that you'd be sent to the kennels after what happened that when Tobias let me out for a run in the garden I slipped through the fence and raced up here to look for you. I'm so pleased you're still here!'

'I am.' I smile, our tails wagging together in perfect timing. 'In fact, I think I'm going to be here for ever now.'

'You are? Oh, that's the best Christmas present I could possibly get! So what happened after we spoke? And how did you convince the Woods to let you stay?'

But before I can answer we're interrupted by a loud banging at the front door.

'What now?' mutters Ben, obviously impatient to get on with lunch.

'Maybe *this* is Father Christmas!' says Emily with excitement.

Ben disappears back into the living room to open the front door again.

'Ah, hello there,' I hear him say, although he doesn't sound particularly pleased to see whoever it is. 'Happy Christmas.'

There's a very non-festive grunt in reply. 'I won't keep you; I'm just looking for my dog.' Instantly recognising the voice, I shrink under the table. 'I saw her disappearing into your garden. I don't suppose she's here?'

'Yes, she's in the kitchen,' says Ben and then adds hesitantly, 'Do come in.'

Moments later he appears at the door, followed by the stooped figure of Tobias.

'Hello, Tobias. Happy Christmas,' says Claire warmly, standing up to greet him.

'Same to you,' he mutters, taking in the festive scene in the kitchen. There's an edge of embarrassment to his usual grumpiness, and I remember Lady telling me that he never went out or spoke to anyone these days. 'I won't keep you. I'll just get Lady and be on my way. Sorry to interrupt your . . .' He waves an arm at the feast on the table.

'Oh please don't worry, it's no problem at all,' says Claire. There's an awkward silence. 'Um, is your daughter visiting you for Christmas?' adds Claire after a moment.

At this a look of pain flickers across Tobias' scowling features. 'No, she . . .' He swallows noisily. 'She passed away earlier this year.'

'Oh God, I'm so sorry,' says Claire, her expression stricken. 'I spoke to her when she visited you once – such a lovely woman. I had no idea.'

'I'm so sorry, Tobias,' says Ben gravely. 'I wish we'd known. If there's anything we can do . . .'

Tobias drops his head as if the weight of his sadness is too much to bear, then after a moment says, 'Thank you. Well, I better be going. Lady, come.'

But she doesn't move. It's not like Lady to be disobedient, and I wonder what she's got in mind.

Tobias calls her again, angrily this time. 'Lady!'

Then I see Claire glance at Ben, as if asking him a question with her eyes, and he gives the slightest of nods in reply.

'Tobias, would you like to join us for lunch?' she asks.

'Oh no, no, I need to get going. Thank you though. *Lady.*'

'But we have all this food, and there's only three of us – well, four if you count Teddy! I don't think you've met our daughter, Emily?'

Tobias grudgingly looks across to where Emily is sitting and his expression suddenly brightens.

'Hello,' says Emily shyly.

And then, amazingly, Tobias finally breaks into a smile, and in that instant his face is transformed. For the first time I get a glimpse of the kind-hearted human who Lady spoke of so warmly. 'Well hello there,' he replies. 'It's lovely to meet you.'

'It's nice to meet you too,' says Emily. 'I thought you might be Father Christmas.'

'Oh no,' says Tobias. 'I'm sorry. I hope you weren't too disappointed.'

'Not really,' says Emily. 'I saw him yesterday.'

Tobias smiles again – 'Well, that's all right then' – but as he looks at Emily, his eyes glisten with tears.

'Tobias?' asks Claire with concern, putting her hand on his arm. 'Are you all right?'

'Yes, I'm sorry, it's just . . .' He rummages in his pocket for a crumpled hanky and dabs at his eyes. 'Emily looks so like my daughter Anne did at that age. It's really quite uncanny. It just took me back, but I'm fine, honestly.'

'Here, come and sit next to me,' says Claire, pulling back a chair. 'We'd really like you to stay for lunch, if you don't have plans. We've been living next door to each other for so long, it would be so nice to finally get to know each other a bit better.'

Tobias hesitates for a moment. 'Well, if you're sure you don't mind . . .'

'Not at all,' says Ben, and I really think he means it. Lady smiles at me, thrilled that Tobias has agreed to stay, and I realise this has probably been her plan all along. She's such a clever dog.

Lunch is just as delicious as I'd hoped, although it turns out that the giant chicken isn't chicken after all, but something called turkey. (It tastes exactly like chicken, though, so I'm in no way disappointed.) And who knew that potatoes could be so delicious? Crunchy on the outside, soft and buttery inside: I'm definitely going to have to add them to my list of favourite foods, somewhere between scrambled eggs and the delicious revelation that is chestnut stuffing. Lady and I gobble down our bowlfuls before our humans have even started theirs (honestly, I'll never cease to be amazed how slowly humans eat) and we lie down together in front of the Aga, where we can keep an eye on how Tobias is getting on.

At first he is rather awkward, as if he's forgotten how to talk to other humans, but by the time they get onto their second helpings (and after a glass or two of that red drink they all like so much) he's been transformed from the sort of man I would scuttle out of the way to avoid into someone I would happily bounce up to, certain of a warm welcome. And, as his face loses that pinched, angry look, he opens up about his daughter and how lonely he's been since she died.

'Anne was such a kind girl: even after she got ill she'd still come up from London to see me whenever she could,' he says. 'I used to live for her visits. Since she died, it sometimes feels like I've lost my reason to go on.'

'I can't imagine how hard it must have been for you,' says Claire. 'Do you have any other family?'

Tobias shakes his head. 'I lost my wife some time ago; Anne was our only child, and I've no brothers or sisters. I've got Lady though, thank goodness. When things were really bad, she gave me a reason to get up every morning.'

'She's a beautiful dog,' says Ben, and they all look over to where we're lying.

'She is, and she's always been a wonderful companion,' says Tobias. 'I'm very lucky. But . . . Oh I don't know, maybe it's because she reminds me of happier times, as Anne loved her almost as much as I did, but I haven't been the best owner recently. There just hasn't seemed to be much to smile about, and poor Lady has had to bear the brunt of my grumpiness.'

'I get grumpy sometimes too,' Emily pipes up. 'I've been ill, you know. Meningitis.'

'Oh poor you,' says Tobias, looking at her in alarm. 'That can be nasty.'

'She's on the mend now though, aren't you, Ems?' says Claire.

Oblivious to Tobias' concern, Emily nods happily. 'Mummy, can I get down and play with Teddy and Lady?'

'Well, we'll be having pudding in a moment, but if nobody else minds?'

'Oh no, not at all,' says Tobias. Then he leans over and adds to Emily, 'All this grown-up chat can get quite boring, can't it?'

'Absolutely,' says Emily, nodding solemnly.

Tobias smiles. 'Perhaps you could look after Lady for me, if you'd like?'

'Absolutely. I'm an excellent dog looker-after, aren't I, Daddy?'

'You are.' Ben laughs. 'One of the best.'

'Well, I'm thrilled that Lady's going to be in such safe hands.' Tobias beams. 'Oh, and if you give her tummy a scratch you'll have a friend for life.'

As Emily comes to join us by the Aga, I keep an ear on the conversation at the table.

'Was she very ill?' asks Tobias softly.

Claire nods. 'We thought we might lose her when she first went into hospital. It's been very hard, and we had another scare just a couple of days ago, but she's a real fighter. The doctors say she'll be fine.'

'Well, thank goodness for that.' Tobias shakes his head sadly. 'It's so hard for a little one to go through an ordeal like that. Was she in hospital for a long time?'

'At first, yes,' says Ben. 'It was weeks. And then when she finally came out, Claire had to care for her at home.'

Tobias turns to her. 'You work in the village, don't you, Claire? At the Bull is it?'

'I did, but I had to take some time off to be with Emily and they . . . replaced me.'

'They sacked her while she was sitting by our daughter's bedside in hospital, wondering if she'd pull through,' says Ben angrily, shaking his head. 'The best head receptionist they'd ever had – they said it them-selves – and they wouldn't even give her a few weeks off. It's disgusting.'

'Shhhh, Ben,' says Claire, nodding towards Emily,

but she's now brushing mine and Lady's coats with her doll's comb – which feels rather relaxing, actually – and obviously isn't listening.

'It's a shame,' Claire goes on, turning back to Tobias. 'I've always enjoyed working, and now that Emily's on the mend I'd like to start again, but there just aren't that many jobs around – certainly not any within walking distance that offer the flexibility I would need until Emily's back at school full time.'

Tobias nods slowly as if he's thinking something over. 'Did you know I used to run the greengrocer's in the village?' he says after a moment. 'I still own it, but I haven't done any of the day-to-day work for years, and the chap who's been keeping it going for me is talking about moving on, so I was planning to sell it. That is, unless . . .' He hesitates, looking shy again. 'I'd completely understand if it's not your sort of thing, Claire, but might you be interested in helping me out in the shop? It would only be part time at first, but there'd be potential to take it over full time . . .'

'Oh my goodness, I would love to!' Claire's face instantly lights up. 'That would be amazing! I mean, I know you'd want to see my CV and have more of a chat before you actually offered me the job, but I'm definitely keen.'

'You know, I really don't think I would,' says Tobias with a smile. 'It's obvious how good you are with people, and if you were at the Bull all that time you're clearly a hard worker. And of course until Emily's back at school you'd be welcome to bring her along while you work. There's a comfy room out the back, and she might even like to help out in the shop.'

Ben reaches for Claire's hand and gives it a squeeze; she turns to him and they beam at each other. Then I remember Ben telling me how he couldn't set up his garden design business until Claire was working again; perhaps this means that he will be able to realise his dream too?

'Thank you so much, Tobias,' says Claire, now looking close to tears. 'I can't tell you how much this will help our family. And I really enjoy cooking, so the idea of working in a greengrocer's is just perfect!'

She leans over to give Tobias a hug, and despite looking rather flustered, he blushes with pleasure.

'Honestly, please don't worry; you'll actually be doing *me* a favour. I'd have to sell the place otherwise. And who knows, if you enjoy the work, perhaps you'd like to buy the shop off me in time? We can see how it goes, anyway.'

'Really, thank you, Tobias.' Ben smiles, reaching across the table to shake his hand. 'All these years we've been living next door to each other, and it takes the dogs to get us talking!'

'Well, thank goodness they did,' says Tobias. 'This has been such a treat for me. You've been ever so kind. You've reminded an old man who'd given up on life how to enjoy himself again.'

'Let's try to do this regularly,' says Claire. 'It would be lovely to have you round for dinner every few weeks. And we'll be seeing much more of you anyway if I'm your new employee!'

'I'll drink to that.' Tobias smiles, raising his glass.

'Cheers,' says Claire, returning the gesture.

'To friendship,' says Ben, 'and new beginnings.'

Lady and I don't get to try the Christmas pudding, but judging by Emily's face when it's served we're not missing out. 'Disgusting,' she mutters as the others tuck in with enthusiasm. Besides, when Claire first brings the pudding to the table the strangest thing happens: even though it's only just come out of the oven, she strikes a match and sets fire to it! At once the pudding is covered with eerie blue flames, but instead of panicking and rushing to put them out, like Ben did once when the *tiniest* spark flew out from the fireplace and landed on the rug, everyone cheers.

I look at Lady, bemused.

'It's a tradition,' she explains. 'Whenever humans do something particularly strange, Teddy, it's usually because of tradition.'

Yet despite the fact that the pudding is probably burned, the grown-ups all seem to enjoy it, even going in for seconds. Instead of the charred pudding Emily has ice cream with some of those tasty gingerbread cookies we made, fragments of which she secretly drops under the table for me and Lady.

When the food is finally finished, Emily starts to fidget. 'Can we please open the presents now? Please please pleeeeeeeease?'

'Yes of course.' Ben smiles. 'You've been very patient.'

'Hooray!' Emily clambers down from her chair, her

movements so much more sure and confident than they were just a week ago. 'Tobias, come with me,' she says, holding out her hand to him in a business-like fashion. 'There are a *lot* of presents to open, so we need to hurry.'

'Ah yes, of course,' he says, his eyes sparkling with amusement. 'Lead the way, Miss Emily.'

Lady and I follow on behind, and I can tell by the bounce in Lady's step and the way she carries her tail high like a flag just how happy she is to see Tobias smile again. The months since Anne's death have been hard for her too, and it must be a huge relief to see him out of the house and enjoying himself.

'Right, Tobias, you sit here,' says Emily, leading him to an armchair by the fire. 'Mummy and Daddy, you go here.' She steers them towards the sofa. 'And Teddy and Lady, you sit with me next to the Christmas tree and all the *presents*!'

Then Emily spots Martha, who has just arrived through the cat flap and is sitting on the doormat doing her usual paw-licking routine while she sizes up what's happening in the room.

'Oh, and Martha, you go next to Mummy and

Daddy.' Emily scoops her up and carries her over to the sofa, clutching her around her middle so her back legs are left dangling. Although she looks rather pained at being carried in such an undignified fashion, Martha doesn't struggle; after Emily has dumped her on the sofa she just starts washing herself again, as if to get over the embarrassment, and then curls up next to Ben and purrs. The room is so full of love and happiness you can almost feel it.

'OK Ems, why don't you hand out the presents?' says Claire, and her daughter dives into the pile under the Christmas tree with a whoop of excitement.

Most of the gifts are for Emily, but Ben gets some gardening books from Claire, which he seems very pleased with, and a bottle of whisky, which is rather less well received.

He looks at the bottle with a sigh. 'It's very kind of Uncle Harold to think of me, but he sends me whisky every year, and every year I write to tell him how grateful I am but that I don't actually drink whisky.'

'Really? That's very a fine bottle,' says Tobias.

Ben looks at him hopefully. 'Are you a whisky drinker?'

'I've been known to have a dram on occasion, yes.' Tobias smiles.

'Well then, you must have it.'

'Oh no, I couldn't possibly . . .'

'Honestly Tobias, we have a cupboard full of Uncle Harold's untouched Christmas whisky.' Claire laughs. 'It would be great to send this particular bottle to a loving home.'

'Well in that case, I would be delighted.' Tobias takes the bottle from Ben and regards the label admiringly. 'I'll enjoy that very much, thank you. Actually, if you don't mind, I might pop home with it now. There's a little something I need to fetch from next door.'

While Tobias is gone, Claire opens her gift from Ben, which is by far the smallest under the tree. I feel a pang of indignation on her behalf; that really is a very tiny present. Surely Ben could have done better?

But when Claire discovers what's inside, her eyes grow huge and her mouth drops open in a way that suggests she's far from disappointed.

'Ben, you shouldn't have!'

Emily cranes to look at it. 'What is it, Mummy?'

'It's the most gorgeous bracelet,' says Claire, holding

up something shiny and sparkly, then putting it on her wrist and admiring it. 'Oh, I *love* it. Thank you!' She throws her arms around Ben. 'You are so naughty. I thought we agreed we wouldn't get each other much for Christmas this year?'

'This isn't so much a Christmas present, as a thank you for everything you've done for our family this year,' says Ben. 'You're been so amazing, my darling, it's the least you deserve.'

They kiss, and although Emily rolls her eyes she can't help but grin at seeing the love between her parents, and after a moment she joins them on the sofa for a hug. As I watch them together, I think back to my first day at Glebe Cottage and how different the Woods family seem today: Emily has more colour in her cheeks and her fighting spirit gets stronger with each day, Ben and Claire appear far less burdened by their worries and have rediscovered hope for the future. All in all, it's a far happier house than it was when I first arrived, and if I've played even a tiny part in that, well, that's the best Christmas present I could ever get.

Just then the door opens and Tobias reappears, taking

his seat back in the armchair. He suddenly looks a little shy, and I notice he's holding a small, slightly worn box.

'Emily, this is for you,' he says. 'It belonged to my daughter Anne when she was a child, but I would love you to have it.'

Emily wriggles off the sofa and comes over to his armchair, taking the box from him and turning it over in her hands.

'It looks very old,' she says.

Tobias laughs. 'It is quite old! It's what you might call an antique. Here, let me help you open it.'

Claire has joined Emily now, and when she sees what's inside she gasps. 'Oh, what a beautiful locket!'

'Is it really for me?' asks Emily in wonder, and when Tobias nods, she grins with delight and throws her arms around him in a hug, making him blush. 'Thank you. I love it!'

'Are you sure, Tobias?' says Claire. 'It really is very generous of you.'

'It's been sitting in a drawer for years,' he says. 'It would make me very happy to see another little girl enjoying it.'

After Claire helps her put it on, Emily goes over to

show Ben the new locket, which is gold-coloured and glitters prettily, and then comes back to where Lady and I are lying by the Christmas tree. Thanks to all the food, I can feel my eyelids growing heavy. Perhaps I'll just have a little nap . . .

'Look, there's one more present under the tree,' Emily is saying. 'Let's see who this one is for . . . Teddy!'

At my name, my head shoots up. For me? All thoughts of sleep instantly forgotten, I hop up and trot over to Emily to have a closer look at the glossy silver box tied with a green ribbon. I can't believe such a smart-looking present is for me! Lady comes to join us too, giving me an excited glance.

'Ems, why don't you help Teddy open it?' says Ben.

So Emily opens the lid and takes out a bright red collar, the exact same colour as Father Christmas's coat with a silvery disc dangling from it covered in writing.

Emily holds it up to show me. 'Look, Teddy, it's got your name on it! teddy woods, glebe cottage – and that's our phone number! Now everyone will know that you're our dog.'

So I'm part of the family, and I have the collar to

prove it! I give a yip of delight and scamper round in a circle. It's official: I'm Teddy Woods!

'Here, let's put it on,' says Claire. 'Teddy, sit!'

This time I don't hesitate: I sit down, my tail wagging so hard it feels like it might never stop, and hold my head up with pride as Claire fastens the collar around my neck. It is surprisingly comfortable and, I imagine, looks rather smart against my white fur. Out of the corner of my eye I see Lady smiling at me.

'Look, there's something else in the box too,' says Claire, taking out a sheet of paper. 'It's a certificate for Teddy. He did such a great job entertaining the children in hospital the other day that the nurses have asked him to become their official children's mascot.'

A look of panic crosses Emily's face. 'But he's still our dog, isn't he?'

'Yes, of course he is, darling, but this means Teddy will be allowed to visit the children's ward every month to cheer up the patients there. It's a very special job, and means Teddy will be able to help lots of children have a happier time in hospital.' She smiles at me. 'We should be extremely proud of him.'

Oh my goodness, this is the most fantastic present

ever, perhaps even better than the squeaky shoe! Apart from snuggling up with Emily, I can't think of anything I'd enjoy more than playing with all those children in hospital. With a howl of glee, I hop up on my hind legs and cover Claire's face with kisses, then bounce over to Emily for more of the same.

'We love you, Teddy,' says Emily, clutching me to her and pressing her cheek into my fur. 'See, Daddy,' she says, looking at Ben. 'I told you he was meant to be our dog.'

'And you were absolutely right, sweetheart.' He smiles. 'Come here, boy.'

He holds out his arms and I jump into them, licking his face ecstatically, and then, seeing as we're now family, I bend down to give the sleeping Martha a big lick as well.

She gives a yowl of protest that makes everyone laugh, but to my delight she doesn't run away.

'Merry Christmas, Martha!' I bark, by now certain that she can understand dog.

And, I might be imagining it, but I'm sure that in reply I see the flicker of a smile in those yellow-green eyes.

Twenty Questions with Daisy Bell

Describe your perfect Christmas Eve.

It would definitely involve snow, and possibly a log cabin and roaring fire as well. A chef would prepare a delicious yet light three-course dinner, while a team of professional present-wrappers would be busy putting the finishing touches to the gifts. There would be old-fashioned parlour games and Christmas carols on repeat (I should probably admit that the reality is nothing like this!).

What is your favorite Christmas tree decoration and why?

That would be the Christmas Wizard. My husband bought him a few years ago as an alternative to the star that usually goes at the top of our tree. I think he's supposed to be Father Christmas, but he has a pointy silver hat and is so skinny that he definitely looks more Gandalf than Santa, hence the name.

What is your favorite part of Christmas day?
Ooh, there are so many! If I had to choose, I'd say it's that glorious moment of anticipation when you sit down in front of a huge plateful of turkey and all those other yummy bits.

What comes first, decorating or gift-wrapping?
Decorating, obviously! Gift-wrapping is the very last thing that happens, usually late on Christmas Eve fuelled by Jamie Oliver's mulled wine recipe.

What is your favorite holiday treat?
Does chestnut stuffing count as a treat? I also love stollen.

What do you have for breakfast on Christmas morning?

My mum does the best Christmas breakfasts: blinis with smoked salmon, coffee and Bucks Fizz. There's nothing better than being a teensy bit drunk at 9 a.m.

Do your family have any specific Christmas traditions?

A month before Christmas we all meet up for 'Stir-up Sunday', when everyone takes a turn to mix the Christmas pudding batter. Our family recipe has been passed down through the generations: it includes lots of chopped nuts for texture and grated apple, which makes the pudding gorgeously moist.

What was your best Christmas ever?

It was probably one when I was a child. I used to get so excited in the run up to Christmas that I'd have to open each door of my advent calendar the night before, as I couldn't wait until morning, so by the time the big day arrived I'd be in such a state of frenzied anticipation that I'd be awake at 1 a.m. to start opening my presents. My poor parents.

What has been the most meaningful Christmas present you have ever received?

My daughter, who was due on Christmas Day but very thoughtfully arrived a few days later, so I still got to enjoy my turkey!

What has been the most meaningful Christmas gift you've ever given?

I bought my husband a very expensive watch for Christmas shortly after we got married. It came packaged in a huge wooden box, and for some reason he assumed it was a beer mug, so when he opened it his face was a picture. As a child I never understood when grown-ups went on about how much nicer it was to give than receive, but now I totally get it.

Did you believe in Father Christmas as a child?

What do you mean? Father Christmas is real, surely!

What is your favorite Christmas film?

Love Actually.

Do you think that Christmas is your favorite holiday of the year?

Absolutely – and I enjoy the build-up to it almost as much as the day itself. I know some people get annoyed when they see Christmas stuff in the shops in October, but I love it.

What is your favorite Christmas song?

I love 'Fairytale of New York' by The Pogues, but I'll always have a special place in my heart for Shakin' Steven's 'Merry Christmas Everyone', primarily because of his dancing and knitwear in the accompanying video.

Do you prefer Christmas in the cold or in a warm climate?

Cold! For me, Christmas isn't really Christmas without snow. As a child, I was absolutely appalled when I learnt that Australians spent Christmas Day on the beach.

What is your favorite Christmas tradition?

Eating until you pass out.

Why is Christmas important to you?
I love the way it brings people together. I know some people find it stressful being with their extended family over Christmas, but although we have our disagreements I really enjoy getting together with my nearest and dearest.

Can you name all nine of Father Christmas's reindeer?
Comet, Cupid, Dancer, Prancer, Blitzen, Vixen, Rudolph . . . and then I had to Google the rest!

If you could have one Christmas wish, what would it be?
It's a cliché, but world peace would be nice.

If you could sum up Christmas for you in three words, what would they be?
Turkey, Tinsel, Togetherness.

Teddy's Favourite Christmas Treats
(only for dogs)

Preparation time: 10 minutes, cooking time: 20 minutes
Makes 30 delicious doggy treats

YOU WILL NEED

320g of whole wheat flour or gluten-free flour

100g of plain rolled oats

60g of grated apple (no seeds)

250g of smooth or crunchy peanut butter

40g of grated carrot

1 tsp of baking powder

One large egg or 60ml of warm water

INSTRUCTIONS

* Pre-heat the oven to 180C, Gas mark 4
* In a medium bowl add the dry ingredients and mix together
* In a small bowl add the remaining ingredients and stir together until combined
* Transfer the contents of the small bowl into the dry ingredients and combine the two until a soft dough is formed
* Lightly dust a work surface with flour and transfer the dough the surface
* Use a rolling pin to roll the dough to roughly 2 cm width
* Use Christmas-themed cookie cutters to cut the dough
* Place the shapes on a lined baking tray and place them in the oven
* After 10 minutes of baking, flip the biscuits and bake for another 10 minutes
* When biscuits are brown and cooked through, remove from oven and allow them to cool for 10 minutes
* Finally, feed to your pampered pooch!

Claire Woods' Marvellous Mince Pies

Preparation time: 50 minutes, cooking time: 20 minutes
Makes 16 pies

YOU WILL NEED
For the pastry

375g plain flour
One large egg
260g soft unsalted butter
One whisked egg or a dash of milk for glazing
Optional: icing sugar for dusting

For the inside

600g shop-bought mincemeat
The zest of one orange

INSTRUCTIONS

* Pre-heat the oven to 180C, Gas mark 4
* Rub together the butter and flour until all the butter is combined, then add the remaining ingredients for the pastry
* Fold the ingredients together until the pastry is formed, wrap the pastry in cling film and place in the fridge for 10–15 minutes to chill
* Mix the zest and the mincemeat in a small bowl
* Once the pastry has chilled, place it on a floured surface and roll the pastry until it is 2–3 mm thick
* Use a circular cookie cutter to create bases for the pies and arrange on a greased muffin tin, pressing the dough down to create a scooped base
* Add 1–2 tbsp of the mince mixture in the centre of each pie
* Roll the remaining pastry to 2–3 mm and use the cutters to cut a circle of dough to place on top of the pie
* Glaze the pies with egg or milk
* Bake for 20 minutes
* Once browned and baked through, remove the pies and leave them to cool for a further 10 minutes
* Dust with icing sugar and serve

Festive Dog Toy
Plaited dog rope

YOU WILL NEED

One old green t-shirt
One old red t-shirt
One old white t-shirt
A small pair of scissors
Three elastic bands

INSTRUCTIONS

★ Cut each t-shirt into three parts, leaving the top 10 cm of the t-shirt uncut

★ Plait each t-shirt from the bottom upwards until you reach the uncut top 10 cm. Temporarily fasten with an elastic band

* Remove the elastic bands and join the uncut 10 cm of each t-shirt together. Tie in a tight knot
* Proceed to plait all three of the different t-shirt strands together to form a larger plait
* Tie off each strand of the plait together to form a knot

The Christmas Jumper

A Christmas jumper: surely the most festive accessory of all? Nicolette Lafonseca, author of *Make Your Own Christmas Jumper*, discusses the recent revival of the Christmas jumper.

Back in the early 2000s, we all laughed as Bridget Jones turned her nose up at Mark Darcy's tasteless reindeer jumper that his mother forced him to wear. We have come a long way since then, and these days he probably wouldn't be the only guest turning up to the party in a novelty knit. In fact, today Bridget would likely be asking why his reindeer jumper did not have any LED lights or sequins on it!

No longer is the Christmas jumper associated only with Bing Crosby at the piano or an embarrassing gift from your granny. Its comeback may have begun as an ironic hipster craze, but the trend has quickly gone mainstream, with a new wave of celebrities in Christmas jumpers flooding our media each year, seen on everyone from pop stars, actors and TV presenters, to sports stars, politicians and even rappers!

We humans are a nostalgic bunch – you need only look at the countless retro and vintage products on sale to realize we are in love with the past. There's something comforting about recapturing things the way they were. Even new technology gets dressed up in grandma's clothes, such as smartphones made to look like 80s cassette tapes, digital cameras that resemble their ancestors, and photo filters that let us transform our sharp modern shots back to the faded snaps of yesteryear. And when it comes to Christmas fashion, the shops are overflowing with jumpers inspired by the ones our elderly relatives used to knit for us, with some retailers reporting festive jumper sales as their financial saviour and others stocking over 30 different styles. We would have been pretty grumpy back then when forced to pull on a homemade monstrosity on Christmas morning, but these days we're positively leaping into our Christmas gear, ready to show it off with pride.

But with the trend rocketing, it is increasingly hard to be different. These days, the only route to a truly unique creation is to avoid buying off the peg like everybody else and instead to create your own. And indeed, there is nothing more rewarding than being able to say, 'I made it myself'.

For more about Christmas jumpers and twenty fun and easy projects you can make at home in a day (even if you can't knit!) check out *Make Your Own Christmas Jumper* by Nicolette Lafonseca. They even have jumpers for dogs!